VIKING

Part of a gilded bronze
harness from Broa, Sweden

Two gold rings

Amber game piece
from Denmark

Resurrection egg

Gold arm-ring
from Denmark

Sword
handle from
Denmark,
9th century

Viking peasant warrior

10th-century figure of man
riding horse, Sweden

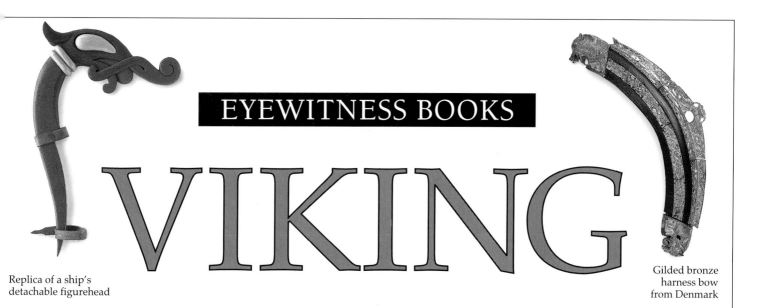

EYEWITNESS BOOKS

VIKING

Replica of a ship's
detachable figurehead

Gilded bronze
harness bow
from Denmark

Written by
SUSAN M. MARGESON

Photographed by
PETER ANDERSON

Belt mount from the
Volga region in Russia

Norwegian Urnes-
style brooch

Thor's hammer

ALFRED A. KNOPF • NEW YORK

The Åby Crucifix,
Denmark, c. 1100

Animal-head post from
the Oseberg ship-burial,
Norway, c. 800–850

A DORLING KINDERSLEY BOOK

Project editor Scott Steedman
Art editor Andrew Nash
Managing editor Simon Adams
Managing art editor Julia Harris
Researcher Céline Carez
Production Catherine Semark
Picture research Julia Ruxton
Editorial consultant David M. Wilson

Silver pendant of a
Viking woman

Silver brooch
from Birka,
Sweden

This is a Borzoi Book published by
Alfred A. Knopf, Inc.

This Eyewitness™ Book has been conceived by
Dorling Kindersley Limited and Editions Gallimard

First American edition, 1994
Copyright © 1994 by Dorling Kindersley Limited, London.
All rights reserved under International and Pan-American
Copyright Conventions. Published in the United States by
Alfred A. Knopf, Inc., New York. Distributed by
Random House, Inc., New York. Published in Great
Britain by Dorling Kindersley Limited, London.

Manufactured in Singapore
0 9 8 7 6 5 4

Danish
coins

Library of Congress Cataloging-in-Publication Data
Margeson, Susan.
Viking / written by Susan Margeson.—1st American ed.
 p. cm.—(Eyewitness books)
Includes index.
1. Vikings—Juvenile literature. 2. Northmen—Juvenile
literature. [1. Vikings] I. Title.
DL65.M356 1994
948'.022—dc20   93-32593
ISBN 0-679-86002-9
ISBN 0-679-96002-3 (lib. bdg.)

Gilded bronze mount from
horse's bridle, Broa, Sweden

Color reproduction by Colourscan, Singapore
Printed in Singapore by Toppan

Bronze key from
Gotland, Sweden

The Jelling Cup

Contents

Gilded copper
weather vane, probably
used on a Viking ship

Who were the Vikings?

FOR 300 YEARS, from the 8th to 11th centuries, the Vikings took the world by storm. In search of land, slaves, gold, and silver, these brave warriors and explorers set sail from their homes in Norway, Sweden, and Denmark. They raided all across Europe, voyaged as far as Baghdad, and even reached America. The speed and daring of Viking attacks became legendary. Christian monks wrote with horror about the violent raids on rich monasteries and towns. But the Vikings were more than wild barbarians from the north. They were shrewd traders, excellent navigators, and superb craftsmen and shipbuilders. They had a rich tradition of story-telling, and lived in a society that was open and democratic for its day.

ROMANTIC VIKINGS
There are many romantic legends about Vikings. Most of them are wrong! Many pictures show them wearing horned helmets. But real Vikings wore round or pointed caps of iron or leather (p. 13).

CATTY BROOCH
A Swedish Viking held his cloak in place with this brooch. It is made of silver coated in gold. The details are highlighted with niello, a black substance like enamel. The style of decoration, with little catlike heads, is known as the Borre style.

SCARY SHIP
Vikings often carved terrifying beasts on their ships to scare their enemies (p. 10). This dragon head was found in a river bed in Holland. It dates from the 5th century, 300 years before the Viking Age. It may have been part of a Saxon warship sunk during a raid. Sailing ships were known before the Vikings, but they were less sophisticated. Viking ships were fast and flexible, and could cruise up narrow channels and inlets with ease.

THE VIKING WORLD
The brown areas on this map are Viking lands and colonies. From late in the 8th century, Vikings raided, traded, and explored far and wide. They discovered Iceland in 870, and sailed further west to Greenland in 985 (pp. 20–21). Leif the Lucky was probably the first European to set foot on America. He is thought to have landed in Newfoundland, Canada, in 1001. In the East, Vikings sailed the Baltic Sea and continued up rivers into Russia. They went overland as far as Constantinople (now Istanbul) and Jerusalem. Vikings also sailed around the west coast of Europe and into the Mediterranean Sea. Thanks to their fast ships and skill at seafaring, they could take people completely by surprise.

Silver wires in the form of plant shoots

AXE OF A CHIEFTAIN
This great iron axehead was found in Mammen, Denmark. It is decorated with silver wires. This side features a glaring human face and a fantastic bird that twists around its own wings, which turn into plant shoots. The Mammen Axe is too beautiful to have been used in battle, and must have been carried by a chieftain to show his power.

Loop so hammer could be worn on chain around neck

THOR'S HAMMER
Vikings believed in many different gods (pp. 52–53). This silver hammer is the sign of the great god Thor. He was said to ride his chariot across the sky, smashing giant snakes with his hammer and making thunder and lightning.

Silver loop for chain

Figure of great bird

GLITTERING SWORD
A strong sword was a Viking's most prized weapon (pp. 14–15). This sword was made and decorated in Norway. Its owner must have died at battle in Ireland, because it was found in a man's grave in Dublin. It is beautifully crafted. The hilt and guard are made of copper decorated with layers of gold and twisted silver and copper wires.

Pommel

Grip, once covered in leather

Guard to protect hand

Helmet with bird's crest and beak

Mustache

Mouth

HERE COME THE VIKINGS!
Ivar the Boneless and his army invaded England in 869. This English manuscript (made 300 years later) shows Ivar's warships arriving at the coast. The first raiders are walking down gangplanks onto the shore. Ivar and his men terrorized the country and killed King Edmund (p. 17).

MYSTERIOUS VIKING FACE
Who is this Viking? A god? A hero from a legend? A warrior? Real pictures of Vikings are very rare. The Vikings didn't have books, and most of the people and animals (pp. 36–37) in their art are imaginary or hard to identify. This small silver head from Aska, Sweden, was worn on a chain as a pendant. It may have been meant to ward off enemies or bring good luck.

Iron blade, now rusted

Lords of the sea

THE VIKINGS WERE SUPERB sailors. Their wooden ships carried them across wild seas, riding the waves, dodging rocks and icebergs. In open seas, the Vikings relied on the ships' big, rectangular sail and navigated by the sun and stars. Their knowledge of seabirds, fish, winds, and wave patterns also helped them find their way. But whenever possible, they sailed within sight of land. To maneuver in coastal waters and rivers, they dropped the mast and rowed the ship instead. Wood rots quickly, so there is little left of most ships. But fortunately a few have survived, thanks to the Viking custom of burying rich people in ships (pp. 54–57). The best preserved are the Oseberg and Gokstad ships from Norway. Both are slender, elegant vessels, light but surprisingly strong.

Stem-post or prow

Ship is made of light oak wood with heavier mast of pine

Sixteen strakes (planks) on each side, each one over-lapping the strake below

Sixteen oar-ports (holes) on each side

Gunwale (top strake)

Keel

GOKSTAD SHIP, FRONT VIEW
One of the grandest Viking ships was found at Gokstad, beside Oslo Fjord (inlet) in Norway. It was excavated in 1880. The elegant lines of the prow and strakes (planks) show the skill of the ship-builders. The ship is 76 ft (23.2 m) long and 17 ft (5.2 m) wide. The keel is a single piece of oak, cut from a tree at least 82 ft (25 m) tall!

DIGGING OUT THE SHIP
The Norwegian ships were preserved by unusual wet conditions. The Gokstad ship sat in a large mound and had a burial chamber on its deck. A man's skeleton lay in the chamber, surrounded by his worldly possessions. He had been buried around 900 A.D.

SAILING TO THE WINDY CITY
The Gokstad ship had 32 shields on each side, painted yellow and black alternately. A full-size replica was sailed across the Atlantic Ocean to Newfoundland and then to Chicago in 1893. It proved how seaworthy the real ship must have been.

LEARNING THE ROPES
Coins and picture stones give clues about how Viking ships were rigged (roped) and sailed. This coin from Birka, Sweden, shows a ship with a furled (rolled-up) sail.

Mast

Mast fish, to lock mast in place

Deck boards

Strakes

Keelson, which runs above keel

Keel

RAISING THE GOKSTAD MAST
The heavy mast was lowered into a groove in the keelson and held in place by the mast fish. The deck boards were loose, so the sailors could store their belongings under them.

HEAVENLY BEDPOST
A mass of everyday objects were buried in the Gokstad ship. These included the dead man's clothes, a cauldron, six wooden cups, a bucket, six beds, three boats, a sledge, tent frames, plus the skeletons of 12 horses, six dogs, and a peacock. One of the beds had two posts carved with animal heads. The dead man wanted to take all his belongings with him to Valhalla, the Viking heaven (p. 53).

Carved tongue

Oak

Sternpost

Proud lion, which would always point away from the wind

Vane was probably mounted on ship's prow along this edge

Copper alloy coated with gold

Figure of "the great beast," like the animal on the Jelling Stone (pp. 60–61)

Lookout

Dragon head

Strakes on hull

Shields

BLOWING IN THE WIND
Weather vanes are used to tell the direction of the wind. This one is from Söderala Church in Sweden. It may once have swung from the prow or mast of a Viking ship. When King Svein Forkbeard's ships left Denmark to conquer England in 1013, a French monk said they glittered with "lions molded in gold" and "birds on the tops of the masts."

BOAT BROOCH
A Danish Viking woman wore this brooch in the 9th century. It is shaped like a ship, with strakes, shields along the side, dragonheads at the prow and stern, and even a lookout atop the mast!

CHANGING COURSE
The steersman held the tiller, a wooden bar that slotted into the top of the steering oar (p. 11). The Gokstad tiller is decorated with a carved animal head.

Leather strap holds oar in place

Tiller

Strakes are held together by iron rivets (p. 25)

Keel, which stops ship from sliding sideways in the wind

GOKSTAD SHIP, STERN VIEW
The Viking ship was steered by a large oar with a long, flat blade. The Gokstad steering oar is 10 ft 10 in (3.3 m) long. The steering oar was always attached to the right side of the ship near the stern, or back. A ship's right side is still called starboard, after the old Norse word *styra* (to steer). The Gokstad ship is symmetrical – the prow, or front, is identical to the stern, except that it has no steering oar.

Steering oar

A Viking warship

THE VIKING WARSHIP was the longest, slenderest, and quickest of Viking vessels, and carried warriors far across the ocean. Like other Viking ships, the warship had a sail and mast, but it could also be rowed. Depending on its size, a warship would have 24 to 50 oars – and carry at least as many warriors. On long voyages, the Viking warriors rowed in shifts. They could glide their ship up narrow inlets and land on any flat beach. Even when it was full, the warship had such a shallow keel that it did not need a landing jetty, and could be unloaded right on the shore. Some warships like the ships on the Bayeux Tapestry (below) could carry horses as well as warriors. When beached, both animals and men would wade ashore. Two well-preserved warships were discovered in the Roskilde Fjord in Denmark. They had been filled with stones and deliberately sunk around the year 1000. One is 92 ft (28 m) from prow to stern, the longest Viking ship ever found.

UNWELCOME GUESTS
A ship full of fierce warriors suddenly landing on the beach filled people with fear and horror. This highly romanticized picture of raiders appeared in a French magazine in 1911.

Dragon made of carved and painted pine wood

Detachable wooden figurehead

DANISH DRAGON SHIP
In 1962, five Viking ships were excavated from Roskilde Fjord in Sjælland, Denmark. They had been scuttled (sunk deliberately), probably to block a channel and protect the harbor from enemy ships. This is a reconstruction of one of the warships. It was 57 ft (17.4 m) long and only 8 ft 6 in (2.6 m) across at the widest point. The ship had seven strakes (planks) on each side, the top three made of ash, the bottom four of oak. There were 12 oar-ports (holes) on each side, so 24 men could row together.

Leather thong holds figurehead in place

Prow · Mast · Stern · Steering oar · Ribs · Side view · Top view

A SHIP AND A HALF
Cross beams and ribs helped to strengthen the hull of a Viking ship. The gaps between the strakes were stuffed with tarred wool. This is called caulking. It kept the water out, and made the ship more flexible in rough seas.

Original rope may have been made of walrus skin

Mooring post

Hull made of seven slender strakes

WILLIAM'S WARSHIP
The Normans were descended from Vikings who settled in Normandy, France. The Bayeux Tapestry, embroidered in the 11th century, describes their conquest of England in 1066. Here the proud ship of the Norman leader William the Conqueror sails toward England. A lookout in the stern blows a horn, while the steersman holds the tiller, attached to the steering oar. The ship has an animal-head prow, and shields line its sides.

Each strake overlaps the one below, in a technique called "clinker" boat-building

FOR THE TILLERMAN
At right is a modern replica of a tiller. It slotted into a hole at the top of the steering oar. The steersman always held the tiller level. By moving it to fore (forward) or aft (backward), he turned the ship to the left or right. The rope would have been tied to a peg in the deck, to stop the tiller from swinging wildly in a storm.

Slot for tiller

Carved and painted wood

Rope made of plant fiber such as hemp

Rigging, the ship's ropes

Sail made of wool or linen, sometimes quilted in stripes or diamond pattern

Lower slot for attaching oar to gunwale

Stern (back)

Steering oar

Prow (front)

In Viking times, this rope would have been made of willow or pine

IN FULL SAIL
This model shows the Roskilde warship in full sail. Viking sails were often dyed blood red, to strike fear into anyone who saw them coming. The shields are slotted into a shield rack that runs along the side of the ship. On other ships, the shields hang from cords.

STEERING OAR
The steering oar was fastened to the gunwale (top strake) by a broad band of leather. Lower down it was also fastened to a wooden boss (knob) on the ship's side with a flexible piece of willow branch or pine root. This allowed the steersman to move the oar easily. In shallow water, he undid the leather band and pulled the oar up.

STRAP-ON
Figureheads and sternposts may have been detachable. This is a replica sternpost. Ships on the beach in the Bayeux Tapestry have holes in their prows where carved and painted dragon heads may have been attached.

Leather thong used to attach sternpost

Flat wooden blade

The warriors would pull out their shields when they fought at sea or landed on a foreign beach

RUNNING WITH THE WIND
These warships are loosely based on the ships found at Gokstad and Oseberg in Norway. With a good wind behind it, a Viking warship was fast. In 1893, the replica of the Gokstad ship took 28 days to sail from Sweden to Newfoundland, Canada.

Shield rack, a long plank behind which the shields could be rested

Gunwale (top strake)

Viking warriors

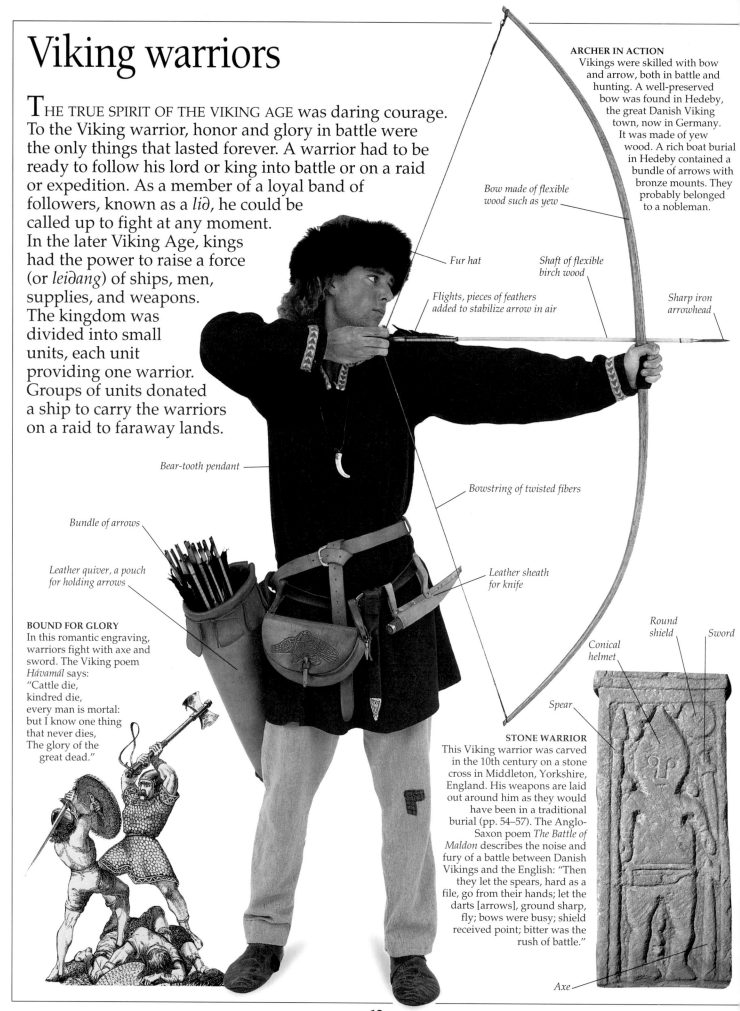

THE TRUE SPIRIT OF THE VIKING AGE was daring courage. To the Viking warrior, honor and glory in battle were the only things that lasted forever. A warrior had to be ready to follow his lord or king into battle or on a raid or expedition. As a member of a loyal band of followers, known as a *lið*, he could be called up to fight at any moment. In the later Viking Age, kings had the power to raise a force (or *leiðang*) of ships, men, supplies, and weapons. The kingdom was divided into small units, each unit providing one warrior. Groups of units donated a ship to carry the warriors on a raid to faraway lands.

ARCHER IN ACTION
Vikings were skilled with bow and arrow, both in battle and hunting. A well-preserved bow was found in Hedeby, the great Danish Viking town, now in Germany. It was made of yew wood. A rich boat burial in Hedeby contained a bundle of arrows with bronze mounts. They probably belonged to a nobleman.

Bow made of flexible wood such as yew

Fur hat

Shaft of flexible birch wood

Flights, pieces of feathers added to stabilize arrow in air

Sharp iron arrowhead

Bear-tooth pendant

Bowstring of twisted fibers

Bundle of arrows

Leather quiver, a pouch for holding arrows

Leather sheath for knife

BOUND FOR GLORY
In this romantic engraving, warriors fight with axe and sword. The Viking poem *Hávamál* says:
"Cattle die,
kindred die,
every man is mortal:
but I know one thing
that never dies,
The glory of the
great dead."

Round shield

Conical helmet

Sword

Spear

STONE WARRIOR
This Viking warrior was carved in the 10th century on a stone cross in Middleton, Yorkshire, England. His weapons are laid out around him as they would have been in a traditional burial (pp. 54–57). The Anglo-Saxon poem *The Battle of Maldon* describes the noise and fury of a battle between Danish Vikings and the English: "Then they let the spears, hard as a file, go from their hands; let the darts [arrows], ground sharp, fly; bows were busy; shield received point; bitter was the rush of battle."

Axe

THE LATEST FASHION
Vikings usually fought on foot. However, in the late 11th century, at the end of the Viking Age, cavalry began to be used in battle. This mounted warrior is from a tapestry woven in Baldishol, Norway, around the year 1200. He is wearing a helmet and chain-mail tunic, and carrying a kite-shaped shield. These longer shields protected the body better than round ones.

Iron spearhead

Iron plates welded together

Chain mail may have hung at the back to protect neck

REAL HELMET (NO HORNS)
The typical Viking helmet was shaped like this one from Gjermundbu in Norway. It has "goggles" to protect the eyes.

Iron helmet with noseguard

Wooden shaft

Chain mail to protect neck

Brooch

Padded leather tunic

Baldric, a strap used to carry a sword

ONE HEAVY SHIRT
These fragments of a chain-mail shirt come from Gjermundbu, Norway. Making chain mail was a slow job. Each iron ring had to be forged separately. Then it was linked to the last one and closed with a rivet or welded in place. It took thousands of rings to make one shirt.

Sword guard to protect hand

Chain-mail tunic, long enough to cover waist

CASUAL DRESS
Unlike Roman legionaries or modern soldiers, Viking warriors didn't wear uniforms. Every soldier had to dress and arm himself. Chieftains wore iron helmets and gear. Poor warriors had to make do with leather clothing, which didn't offer as much protection as chain mail. Leather tunics were worn instead, and leather caps were more common than iron helmets. Shields of wood and iron were a Viking's main defense against arrows and blows from axes or swords.

Iron sword

Tweed trousers

Sheath for sword

Wooden shield with iron boss (stud)

Men probably wore woolen socks, like one found in York, England

Leather shoes, often made of goat skin

Weapons

HIS SPEAR, HIS AXE, his shield, and especially his sword – these were a warrior's most prized possessions. In poems and sagas (pp. 52–53), swords were given names celebrating the strength and sharpness of the blade or the glittering decoration of the hilt (handle). Weapons were made of iron, and often decorated with inlaid or encrusted silver or copper. A beautifully ornamented sword was a sign that the owner was rich or powerful. Before the arrival of Christianity, a Viking's weapons were usually buried with him when he died. Helmets (p. 13) are rarely found, because most of them were made of leather and have rotted away.

Notch to cut feathers

Broad iron blade

Wooden board about 3 ft (1 m) in diameter

Leather binding to protect the edges

ARROWS
Arrows were used for hunting as well as for battle (p. 12). These iron arrowheads from Norway would have been lashed to shafts of birch wood. The two on the right were used to hunt reindeer. The other one was designed for killing birds.

THRUSTING AND THROWING
Spears were mainly used as thrusting weapons, and had large broad blades. The sockets were often decorated. Throwing spears had much lighter, narrower blades, so they would fly straight and true.

Geometric patterns of copper and silver

Wooden shaft was riveted into socket

BERSERK
Tyr was the Viking god of war. In this romantic engraving he has a shaggy bearskin cloak, with the bear's head worn as a helmet. Warrior called *berserkir* prepared for battle by putting on bearskin cloak or shirts and working themselves into a frenzy. This was called going *berserk*, from the Old Norse word meaning "bear shirt."

Iron thrusting spearhead from Ronnesbæksholm, Sjælland, Denmark

Iron throwing spearhead from Fyrkat fortress, Jutland, Denmark

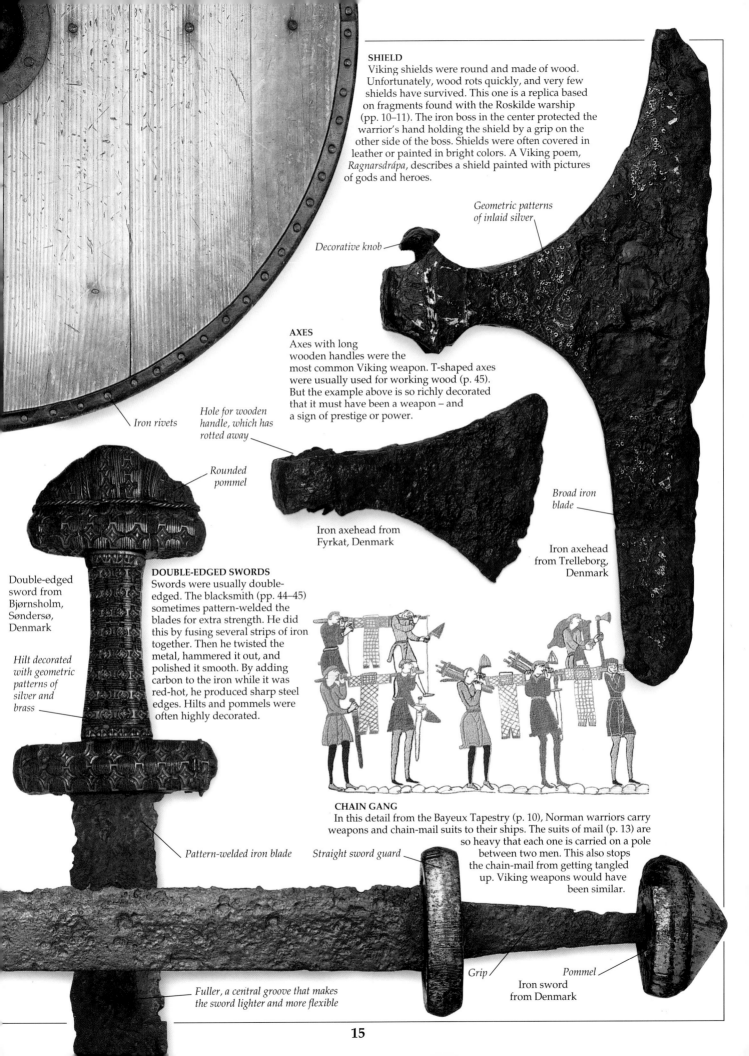

SHIELD

Viking shields were round and made of wood. Unfortunately, wood rots quickly, and very few shields have survived. This one is a replica based on fragments found with the Roskilde warship (pp. 10–11). The iron boss in the center protected the warrior's hand holding the shield by a grip on the other side of the boss. Shields were often covered in leather or painted in bright colors. A Viking poem, *Ragnarsdrápa*, describes a shield painted with pictures of gods and heroes.

Geometric patterns of inlaid silver

Decorative knob

AXES

Axes with long wooden handles were the most common Viking weapon. T-shaped axes were usually used for working wood (p. 45). But the example above is so richly decorated that it must have been a weapon – and a sign of prestige or power.

Hole for wooden handle, which has rotted away

Iron rivets

Rounded pommel

Broad iron blade

Iron axehead from Fyrkat, Denmark

Iron axehead from Trelleborg, Denmark

Double-edged sword from Bjørnsholm, Søndersø, Denmark

Hilt decorated with geometric patterns of silver and brass

DOUBLE-EDGED SWORDS

Swords were usually double-edged. The blacksmith (pp. 44–45) sometimes pattern-welded the blades for extra strength. He did this by fusing several strips of iron together. Then he twisted the metal, hammered it out, and polished it smooth. By adding carbon to the iron while it was red-hot, he produced sharp steel edges. Hilts and pommels were often highly decorated.

CHAIN GANG

In this detail from the Bayeux Tapestry (p. 10), Norman warriors carry weapons and chain-mail suits to their ships. The suits of mail (p. 13) are so heavy that each one is carried on a pole between two men. This also stops the chain-mail from getting tangled up. Viking weapons would have been similar.

Pattern-welded iron blade

Straight sword guard

Grip

Pommel

Iron sword from Denmark

Fuller, a central groove that makes the sword lighter and more flexible

Terrorizing the West

THE VIKINGS SWEPT into western Europe, terrorizing towns along the coast, plundering churches, and grabbing riches, slaves, and land. The first recorded raid, on the famous monastery of Lindisfarne in 793, shocked the whole Christian world. From then on, attacks all over Europe intensified. Bands of Viking warriors roamed the North Sea and the English Channel, raiding choice targets at will. Soon the Vikings were venturing further inland. They sailed up the great rivers of Europe – the Rhine, Seine, Rhone, and Loire – and even overran Paris. The raiders began to spend the winters in areas they had captured. Then they set up bases to attack other targets. The Vikings often demanded huge payments for leaving an area in peace. Some warriors were off raiding for years. Björn Jarnsmiða and his companion Hasting spent three years with 62 ships in Spain, North Africa, France, and Italy. They lost a lot of their treasure in storms on the way home.

Lead weight with animal head made in Ireland

THROWN INTO THE THAMES
This Viking sword was found in the River Thames in London. This big English city was attacked many times, once by 94 ships. But it was never taken.

SOUVENIR OF PARIS
Paris was conquered on Easter Sunday, March 28, 845. Charles the Bald, the French king, had to pay the raiders 7,000 lb (3,175 kg) of silver to get peace. The Viking leader Ragnar even took a bar from the city gate as a souvenir. But he and most of his men died of disease on their way back to Scandinavia.

Rusted iron blade

HOLY SLAUGHTER
Lindisfarne is a small island off the east coast of England. The celebrated monastery there was destroyed by Vikings in 793. These warriors on a stone from the island may well be the Viking raiders. The *Anglo-Saxon Chronicle*, a contemporary English historical record, reported: "the ravages of heathen men miserably destroyed God's church on Lindisfarne, with plunder and slaughter."

RAIDING FRANCE
This picture of a Viking ship is in a French manuscript from around 1100. Viking ships attacked French towns and monasteries all through the 9th century. One group of Vikings settled in the Seine region. Another band under the chieftain Rollo made their homes around Rouen. This area became known as Normandy, "Land of the Northmen" (p. 10).

KILLING THE KING

King Edmund was king of East Anglia in England in 869. This 12th-century manuscript shows him being beaten by Vikings. Then they tied him to a tree and shot him full of arrows. He still refused to give up his belief in Christ, so they cut his head off. The Vikings later settled in East Anglia under their leader King Guthrum.

Interlace designs, typical of Dublin Viking art

IRISH CROOK

Raids on Ireland began in 795. By the 820s the Vikings had worked their way around the entire island. The town of Dublin became a thriving Viking trading center with links to many other countries. This wooden animal head comes from a crook or walking stick. It was made in Dublin early in the 11th century.

SCOTCHED

This is a painting of the Viking invasion of Scotland. Many of the raiders were Norwegians who came via the Shetland and Orkney Islands. From these resting places, the many Hebridean islands, the Isle of Man (pp. 37, 51), and Ireland were all within easy reach.

DEATH OF THE ARCHBISHOP

In 1011 Archbishop Alphege of Canterbury was seized by Vikings who were raiding the English countryside. They were angry because the English King Ethelred hadn't paid them fast enough. The archbishop refused to be ransomed. The Vikings, who were very drunk, pelted him with bones and the skulls of cattle. He was finally killed with a battle-axe.

RANVAIK'S SHRINE

This shrine or casket was made in Scotland or Ireland in the 8th century. It holds holy Christian relics. It was probably taken to Norway as loot. There the new owner inscribed a message in runes (pp. 58–59) on the bottom: "Ranvaik owns this casket."

Hollow box of yew wood covered in plates of tin and copper mixed with other metals

Small pieces of red enamel

Whole casket is shaped like a house

East into Russia

A SHORT SAIL ACROSS THE BALTIC SEA is all that separates Scandinavia from the rivers of Russia. Viking warriors and traders sailed into the Dniepr and Volga rivers and followed them all the way to the Black and Caspian seas. From there, the great and mysterious cities of Constantinople (heart of the Byzantine Empire) and Baghdad (capital of the Islamic world) were within easy reach. The history of Viking raids in the East is not as well recorded as in western Europe. But all through Russia and beyond, Vikings left brooches, weapons, and runic inscriptions that trace their travels. Traders swapped Siberian furs for silk, spices, and Arab silver. Viking warriors were even hired as Imperial guards in Constantinople.

VIKING GRAFFITI
This stone lion once stood in the Greek port of Piraeus. A Viking traveler inscribed it with long looping bands of runes, the Scandinavian writing (pp. 58–59). Much later, in 1687, Venetian soldiers carried the lion off to Venice. The runes have eroded too much to be read today. Still, such "graffiti" is often the only evidence of where Vikings traveled.

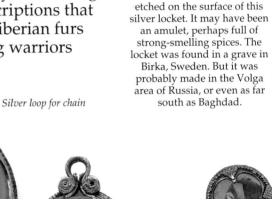

TREE OF LIFE
An Oriental tree of life is etched on the surface of this silver locket. It may have been an amulet, perhaps full of strong-smelling spices. The locket was found in a grave in Birka, Sweden. But it was probably made in the Volga area of Russia, or even as far south as Baghdad.

Silver loop for chain

EASTERN FASHIONS
Gotland is an island in the Baltic Sea. Gotland Vikings traveled far into Russia, and their excellent craftsmen often adopted styles from the East. These beads and pendant are made of rock crystal set in silver. They were probably made in Gotland, where they were found. But the style is distinctly Slav or Russian.

High-quality rock crystal shaped like a convex lens

CHECKERED PAST
This silver cup was made in the Byzantine Empire in the 11th century. It was taken back to Gotland by Vikings, who added a name and a magical inscription on the bottom in runes. The cup was buried around 1361, and found by ditch-diggers in 1881.

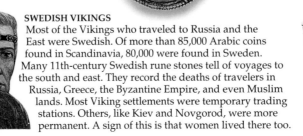

SWEDISH VIKINGS
Most of the Vikings who traveled to Russia and the East were Swedish. Of more than 85,000 Arabic coins found in Scandinavia, 80,000 were found in Sweden. Many 11th-century Swedish rune stones tell of voyages to the south and east. They record the deaths of travelers in Russia, Greece, the Byzantine Empire, and even Muslim lands. Most Viking settlements were temporary trading stations. Others, like Kiev and Novgorod, were more permanent. A sign of this is that women lived there too.

Birds, leaves, and winged lions

Fur hat

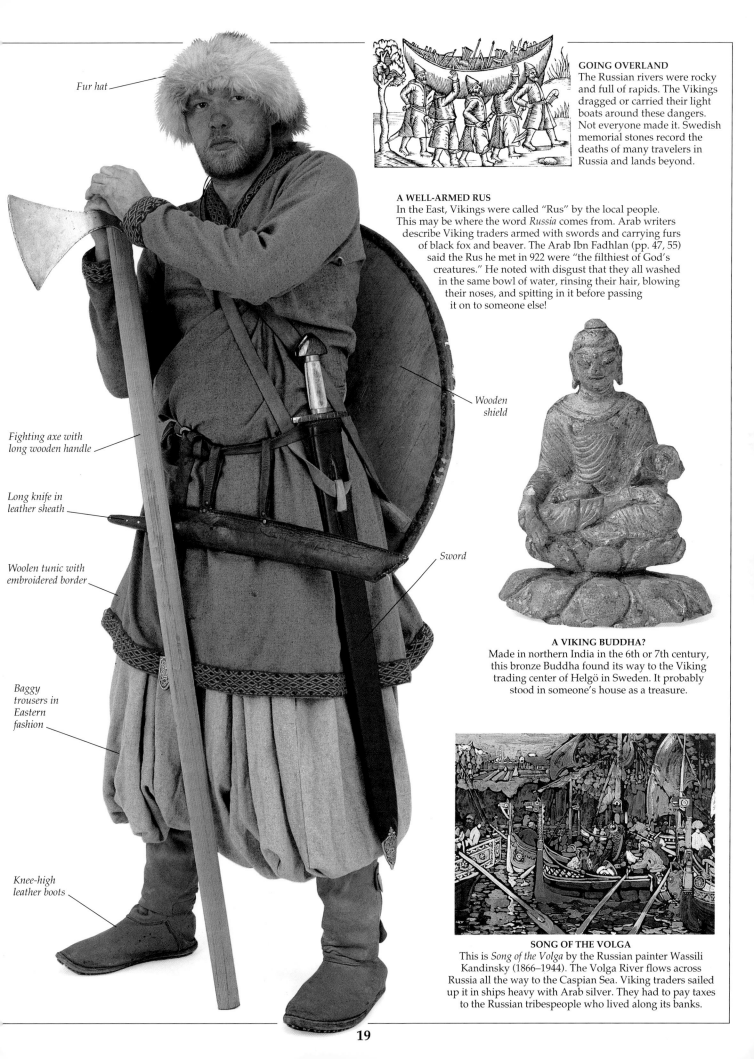

GOING OVERLAND
The Russian rivers were rocky and full of rapids. The Vikings dragged or carried their light boats around these dangers. Not everyone made it. Swedish memorial stones record the deaths of many travelers in Russia and lands beyond.

A WELL-ARMED RUS
In the East, Vikings were called "Rus" by the local people. This may be where the word *Russia* comes from. Arab writers describe Viking traders armed with swords and carrying furs of black fox and beaver. The Arab Ibn Fadhlan (pp. 47, 55) said the Rus he met in 922 were "the filthiest of God's creatures." He noted with disgust that they all washed in the same bowl of water, rinsing their hair, blowing their noses, and spitting in it before passing it on to someone else!

Fighting axe with long wooden handle

Long knife in leather sheath

Woolen tunic with embroidered border

Baggy trousers in Eastern fashion

Knee-high leather boots

Wooden shield

Sword

A VIKING BUDDHA?
Made in northern India in the 6th or 7th century, this bronze Buddha found its way to the Viking trading center of Helgö in Sweden. It probably stood in someone's house as a treasure.

SONG OF THE VOLGA
This is *Song of the Volga* by the Russian painter Wassili Kandinsky (1866–1944). The Volga River flows across Russia all the way to the Caspian Sea. Viking traders sailed up it in ships heavy with Arab silver. They had to pay taxes to the Russian tribespeople who lived along its banks.

Discovering new lands

THE VIKINGS WERE DARING EXPLORERS. In search of new land, they sailed their slender ships into the frozen, uncharted waters of the North Atlantic. Most of the explorers came from Norway, where the valleys were crowded and farmland was scarce. They discovered the Faroe Islands, Iceland, far-off Greenland, and "Vinland" (America). As reports of these exciting discoveries got back to Scandinavia, ships full of eager settlers set sail. Between 870 and 930, for example, more than 10,000 Vikings arrived in Iceland. They found empty spaces, wild forests, and seas teeming with fish. The sea voyages were long and dangerous, and many ships were lost in storms. But the urge to travel to new lands never dimmed.

RED AND GREEN LAND
A man called Gunnbjörn found Greenland after his ship was blown off course in a storm. The huge island was explored in 984 and 985 by Erik the Red, a chief who had been accused of murder and forced to leave Iceland. Erik encouraged hundreds of Icelanders to settle in Greenland.

THE THINGVELLIR
Iceland is a volcanic island. This high plain surrounded by great cliffs of lava was chosen as the site for the Althing, the governing assembly, which met once a year in the open air (p. 29). It is thought to have first met in 930.

Iceland

Iceland was discovered in 870. In good weather it took seven days to get there from Norway. The first settler was Ingolf, from Sunnfjord, Norway. He built a large farm on a bay overlooking the sea. This later became the capital, Reykjavik. The settlers raised sheep, and used local iron and soapstone to make weapons and cooking pots. Soon they were exporting these natural resources, along with woolen and linen cloth.

REINDEER KILLS REINDEER
These arrowheads from Greenland are carved from reindeer antler. Iron was very scarce, so weapons had to be made from the materials at hand. Reindeer were a major source of food, and the settlers may have used these arrows to hunt them.

FIRE AND ICE LAND
Iceland's interior is harsh and inhospitable, with jagged mountains, glaciers, and several active volcanoes. But the coast is green and fertile. In the Viking Age there were also extensive forests between the mountains and the sea. By A.D. 930 the coast was densely populated. The interior was never really inhabited.

West Fjords

Faxa Fjord

Reykjavik

Thingvellir (Thing Plain)

Mt. Hekla (volcano)

Vatna Jökull (huge glacier)

HELGE'S ANIMALS
This elegant piece of carved wood was discovered in the ruins of a house in Greenland. It dates from the 11th century. It may be the arm of a chair, or a tiller used to steer a boat (pp. 9, 11). The surface is carved with big-eyed animals that look like cats. A runic inscription at the end probably proclaims the owner's name, Helge.

America

Leif the Lucky, Erik the Red's son, also discovered land by accident when his ships went off course on a trip to Greenland. Around the year 1001, he became the first European to set foot on North America, probably in Newfoundland, Canada. He called it Vinland, "Wine Land." This strange name may come from giant huckleberries that Leif thought were red grapes. The Vikings also discovered Markland ("Wood Land") and Helluland ("Rock Land"). These may be Labrador and Baffin Island to the north.

VIKINGS IN VINLAND
Only one Viking settlement has been found in North America. This is at L'Anse aux Meadows (above) in Newfoundland. Large houses with thick turf walls have been unearthed. Only two Viking objects, a dress pin and a spindle whorl (p. 44), have turned up. Despite the fertile land and mild climate, the Viking settlements didn't last long. They were a long way from home, and the local people were hostile.

Modern tapestry showing Leif the Lucky sighting Vinland

EXPLORING THE FROZEN NORTH
This rune stone was found at Kingiktorsuak, Greenland, at latitude 73° North. This means that settlers must have explored the frozen north of the island. The stone was carved around the year 1300. The Viking community in Greenland died out not too long after this date.

GREENLAND INUIT
The Inuit (Eskimos) made everything they needed from the natural resources of the land and sea. But the Vikings had to import timber, iron, and corn to survive.

Greenland

Most of this inhospitable island is covered in ice and snow. Erik the Red called it "Greenland" to encourage people to move there. The Vikings made two settlements, the eastern and western settlements, in the two areas where the land could be farmed. They built their farms on the edges of fjords, often far inland. They farmed sheep and cattle, but depended mainly on reindeer and seals for food.

WHALEBONE AXE
The Inuit in Greenland made weapons from the bones of seals, whales, and reindeer. This whalebone axehead from a Viking farm shows that the Vikings did the same. Its shape is very similar to iron axeheads (p. 15), but it wouldn't have been as strong. It was probably a toy made for a child.

Animal head

Animal with gaping jaws and huge teeth

A Viking fort

THE VIKINGS BUILT FOUR great circular forts in Denmark. Two of them, at Aggersborg and Fyrkat, are on the Jutland peninsula. The other two are at Trelleborg on the island of Sjælland and Nonnebakken on the island of Fyn. It was thought that King Svein Forkbeard built them to help launch his invasion of England in 1013. But dendrochronology – a dating method based on the growth rings in trees – shows that the forts were built earlier, around 980. It is now thought that King Harald Bluetooth had them constructed to unify his kingdom and strengthen his rule. Bones dug up in cemeteries outside the ramparts prove that women and children lived there as well as men. Some of the fort buildings were workshops, where smiths forged weapons and jewelry from gold, silver, and iron.

THE WALLS GO UP
The first step in building a fort was clearing the land and preparing the timber. This detail from a 15th-century Byzantine manuscript shows Swedish Vikings making the walls of Novgorod in Russia in the 10th century.

Aerial photograph of the site of the Trelleborg fortress

TRELLEBORG, FROM THE AIR
The forts had a strict geometrical layout. Each one lay within a high circular rampart, a mound of earth and turf held up by a wooden framework. This was divided into four quadrants by two roads, one running north–south, the other east–west. Four long houses sat in a square in each of the quadrants. The roads were paved with timber. Covered gateways, which may have been topped with towers, were placed where the roads met the rampart. The largest fort, Aggersborg, was 790 ft (240 m) in diameter. Trelleborg was much smaller, 445 ft (136 m) across. Trelleborg is unusual because 15 extra houses were built outside the main fort. These were protected by their own rampart. All four forts were built on important land routes, possibly so that Harald could keep an eye on the area in case of rebellion.

Two roads criss-crossing fort

River

Cemetery

Houses

Circular ramparts built of earth and turf and faced with wood

Extra outer rampart

Ditch

Four houses around a square yard

Layout of the Trelleborg fortress

TRELLEBORG HOUSE, SIDE VIEW
The buildings at the forts were made of wood, which rotted away a long time ago. All that is left are ghostly outlines and black holes where the posts once stood. This replica of a house was built in 1948. It is 96 ft 5 in (29.4 m) long. The elegant curving roof is "hogbacked" in shape. House-shaped gravestones and caskets from England give an idea of how it once looked. Experts now believe that there was only one roof that reached all the way down to the short outer posts.

Iron blade, badly rusted now

Silver inlaid in geometric patterns

Gables decorated with projections called finials

THE COMPLETE WORKS OF HARALD BLUETOOTH

The four forts were only one of King Harald Bluetooth's huge projects that left his mark on the Danish landscape. His engineering works include the first bridge in Scandinavia, a huge wooden structure at Ravning Enge in Jutland. He also strengthened the Danevirke, a massive wall that protected Denmark from invasion from the south. And he built a grand memorial at Jelling in Jutland (above). This includes the Jelling Stone, the biggest and grandest of Viking memorial stones (pp. 60–61).

GUARDING THE FORT

Various weapons have been found at the forts. This beautiful T-shaped axehead (p. 15) comes from a grave at Trelleborg. It was probably a symbol of power, not a working weapon. A light throwing spear was found in a guardhouse at the Fyrkat fortress.

TRELLEBORG HOUSE, FRONT VIEW

The houses were built of upright staves (wooden planks) set straight into the earth. They all followed a standard pattern. The main door at each end opened into a small room. These led in turn into a huge central living room where a big fire always burned. Farm-houses like the ones excavated at Vorbasse in Jutland have a similar layout. The wood must have rotted quickly, and there is no evidence of repairs. The forts were probably only inhabited for a few years. King Harald was forced into exile in 986. Soon after this date, the forts he had built were left to rot.

Sturdy wooden posts hold up roof

Walls made of staves (planks)

Main door

Smoke hole over fire that burned in a hearth in the middle of the central living room

Roof is covered in overlapping shingles (wooden tiles)

Finials

Other ships

THE VIKINGS BUILT SHIPS and boats of many shapes and sizes, suited to different waters and uses. They were all variations on the same design, with overlapping strakes (planks), a keel, and matching prow and stern. Only the longest, fastest vessels were taken raiding. Cargo ships were slower and wider, with lots of room for storing goods. Other boats were specially made for sailing in narrow inlets and rivers, for following the coast, or for crossing oceans. There were fishing boats, ferries for carrying passengers across rivers and fjords, and small boats designed for lakes. Small rowing boats were also carried on board larger boats.

BRONZE AGE BOATS
Rock carvings in Sweden and Norway show boats from as early as 1800 B.C. Sails were developed in Scandinavia just before the Viking Age, around A.D. 700. Before then, all ships were rowed.

LEIF SIGHTS AMERICA
Explorers sailed wide-bodied, sturdy ships. These were much heavier than warships and had more space for passengers and their belongings and supplies. In this dramatic interpretation of Leif the Lucky's voyage to America (p. 21), Leif is shown pointing in wonder at the new continent. His other hand holds the tiller. The raised deck at the stern (back) can be clearly seen. Leif was Erik the Red's son (p. 20), and is also known as Leif Eriksson.

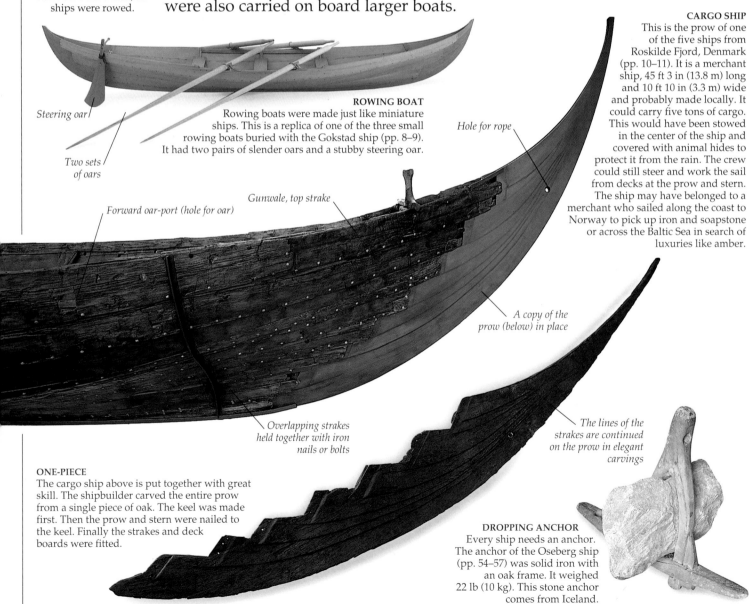

Steering oar

ROWING BOAT
Rowing boats were made just like miniature ships. This is a replica of one of the three small rowing boats buried with the Gokstad ship (pp. 8–9). It had two pairs of slender oars and a stubby steering oar.

Two sets of oars

Forward oar-port (hole for oar)

Gunwale, top strake

Hole for rope

CARGO SHIP
This is the prow of one of the five ships from Roskilde Fjord, Denmark (pp. 10–11). It is a merchant ship, 45 ft 3 in (13.8 m) long and 10 ft 10 in (3.3 m) wide and probably made locally. It could carry five tons of cargo. This would have been stowed in the center of the ship and covered with animal hides to protect it from the rain. The crew could still steer and work the sail from decks at the prow and stern. The ship may have belonged to a merchant who sailed along the coast to Norway to pick up iron and soapstone or across the Baltic Sea in search of luxuries like amber.

A copy of the prow (below) in place

The lines of the strakes are continued on the prow in elegant carvings

Overlapping strakes held together with iron nails or bolts

ONE-PIECE
The cargo ship above is put together with great skill. The shipbuilder carved the entire prow from a single piece of oak. The keel was made first. Then the prow and stern were nailed to the keel. Finally the strakes and deck boards were fitted.

DROPPING ANCHOR
Every ship needs an anchor. The anchor of the Oseberg ship (pp. 54–57) was solid iron with an oak frame. It weighed 22 lb (10 kg). This stone anchor comes from Iceland.

ROAR EGE, FRONT VIEW

Named *Roar Ege*, this is a replica of the merchant ship from Roskilde on the opposite page. It was built to see how much cargo the ship could hold and how many men were needed to sail it. The ship has oars, but the crew of four to six only use them for maneuvering in tight spots. Usually they rely on the large sail. In good winds, *Roar Ege* averages 4 knots or nautical miles per hour (4.6 mph), and has reached 8 knots (9.3 mph). The ship was ideally suited to sailing in the Baltic Sea and Danish coastal waters, and may have been taken up rivers or into the North Sea.

Mooring post

High prow, which stops ship from nose-diving in rough water

THE OSEBERG SHIP

One of the most beautiful Viking vessels is the Oseberg ship (pp. 54–57). It was not as sturdy as the Gokstad ship, and was probably built to cruise coastal waters. This is a scene from the ship's excavation.

RIVETING STUFF

Iron rivets held the strakes together. Often they are all that is left of a ship once the wood has rotted away.

SETTLERS' VESSEL

This is a model of a sturdy cargo ship with a square sail and shrouds (ropes) securing the mast. Ships like this carried settlers to Iceland and Greenland.

Each side has three oar-ports, two near the prow and one at the stern

Pronounced keel, needed for sailing

OUT OF TUNE

The remains of another large ship were found at Tune, across the Oslo Fjord from the Gokstad and Oseberg ship mounds. The Tune ship (above) is built of oak, with a pine steering oar and cross-beams. It was about 66 ft (20 m) long, a little shorter than the Gokstad ship.

INSIDE *ROAR EGE*

This view inside the stern shows how Viking ships were built. The hull, or outside, was built first. This was then strengthened with cross-beams secured to the strakes with curved "knees." The top layer of cross-beams could support decks or rowing benches.

Sternpost, almost identical to prow

Hull, made of eight strakes

Knee

Top of two levels of cross-beams

Stringer, a horizontal strengthener

Stern oar-port

Trading east and west

THE VIKINGS WERE GREAT TRADERS who traveled far beyond Scandinavia buying and selling goods. The riches of the North included timber for ship-building; iron for making tools and weapons; furs for warm clothing; skins from whales and seals for ship ropes; and whale bones and walrus ivory for carving. These were carried to far-flung places and exchanged for local goods. Traders would return from Britain with wheat, silver, and cloth, and bring wine, salt, pottery, and gold back from the Mediterranean. They sailed across the Baltic Sea and upriver into Russia, then continued on foot or camel as far as Constantinople (now Istanbul) and Jerusalem. In markets all along the way, they haggled over the price of glass, exotic spices, silks, and slaves. Some Viking market towns grew to be important trade centers, such as Birka in Sweden, Kaupang in Norway, Hedeby in Denmark, York in England, Dublin in Ireland, and Kiev in Ukraine.

THE SLAVE TRADE
Some Vikings made their fortune trading slaves. They took many Christian prisoners, like this 9th-century French monk. Some slaves were taken home for heavy farm and building work. Others were sold for silver to Arab countries.

Coin and die for striking (making) coins, from York, England

Three early Danish coins

THE COMING OF COINS
Coins only became common toward the end of the Viking Age. Before then, goods were usually bought with pieces of silver or bartered – swapped for items of similar value. The first Danish coins were made in the 9th century. But it wasn't until 975, under King Harald Bluetooth, that coins were made in large numbers.

Brass Buddha-like figure

Colorful enamel

Bands of brass

MADE IN ENGLAND?
One of the many beautiful objects found with the Oseberg ship (pp. 54–57) was the mysterious "Buddha bucket." Its handle is attached to two brass figures with crossed legs that look just like Buddhas. But the Vikings were not Buddhists, and the craftsmanship suggests that the figures were made in England. So how did the splendid bucket end up in a queen's grave in Norway? It must have been traded and brought back from England.

Staves (strips) of yew wood

RHINE GLASS
Only rich Vikings drank from glass cups. Many have been found in Swedish graves. This glass must have been bought or stolen in the Rhineland, in modern Germany.

TUSK, TUSK
The Vikings hunted walruses for their hide, which was turned into ship ropes. The large animals were skinned in a spiral, starting from the tail. Traders also sold the animal's ivory tusks, either unworked or beautifully carved.

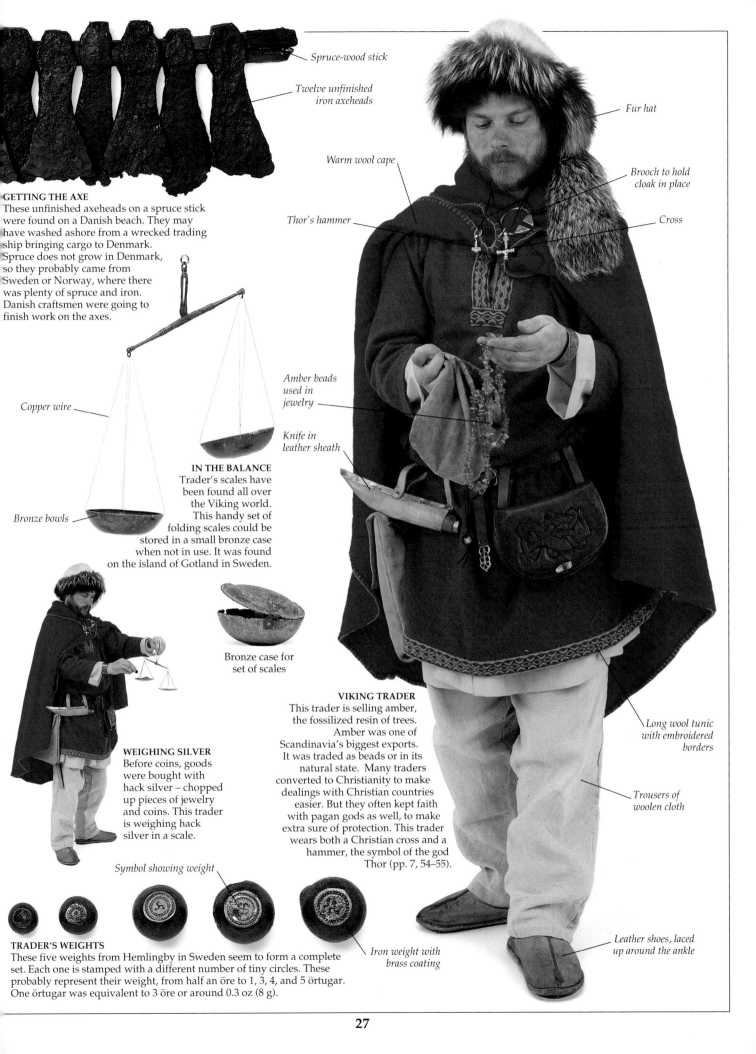

Spruce-wood stick

Twelve unfinished
iron axeheads

GETTING THE AXE
These unfinished axeheads on a spruce stick
were found on a Danish beach. They may
have washed ashore from a wrecked trading
ship bringing cargo to Denmark.
Spruce does not grow in Denmark,
so they probably came from
Sweden or Norway, where there
was plenty of spruce and iron.
Danish craftsmen were going to
finish work on the axes.

Copper wire

IN THE BALANCE
Trader's scales have
been found all over
the Viking world.
This handy set of
folding scales could be
stored in a small bronze case
when not in use. It was found
on the island of Gotland in Sweden.

Bronze bowls

Bronze case for
set of scales

WEIGHING SILVER
Before coins, goods
were bought with
hack silver – chopped
up pieces of jewelry
and coins. This trader
is weighing hack
silver in a scale.

Symbol showing weight

TRADER'S WEIGHTS
These five weights from Hemlingby in Sweden seem to form a complete
set. Each one is stamped with a different number of tiny circles. These
probably represent their weight, from half an öre to 1, 3, 4, and 5 örtugar.
One örtugar was equivalent to 3 öre or around 0.3 oz (8 g).

Iron weight with
brass coating

Fur hat

Warm wool cape

Brooch to hold
cloak in place

Thor's hammer

Cross

Amber beads
used in
jewelry

Knife in
leather sheath

VIKING TRADER
This trader is selling amber,
the fossilized resin of trees.
Amber was one of
Scandinavia's biggest exports.
It was traded as beads or in its
natural state. Many traders
converted to Christianity to make
dealings with Christian countries
easier. But they often kept faith
with pagan gods as well, to make
extra sure of protection. This trader
wears both a Christian cross and a
hammer, the symbol of the god
Thor (pp. 7, 54–55).

Long wool tunic
with embroidered
borders

Trousers of
woolen cloth

Leather shoes, laced
up around the ankle

Kings and freemen

WELL-GROOMED
The well-off Viking warrior or chieftain took pride in his appearance. This Viking carved from elk antler has neatly trimmed hair and beard.

VIKING SOCIETY HAD THREE CLASSES – slaves, freemen, and nobles. Most of the hard labor was done by slaves, or *thralls*. Many were foreigners captured in war (p. 26). Wealthy people sometimes had their slaves killed and buried with them. Slaves could be freed. Freemen included farmers, traders, craftsmen, warriors, and big landowners. At the beginning of the Viking Age, there were many local chieftains (nobles) who ruled over small areas. They were subject to the rule of the Thing, the local assembly where all freemen could voice their opinions and complain about others. But chieftains and kings gradually increased their wealth and power by raiding and conquering foreign lands. By the end of the Viking Age, around A.D. 1050, Norway, Denmark, and Sweden were each ruled by a single, powerful king, and the role of the Things had declined.

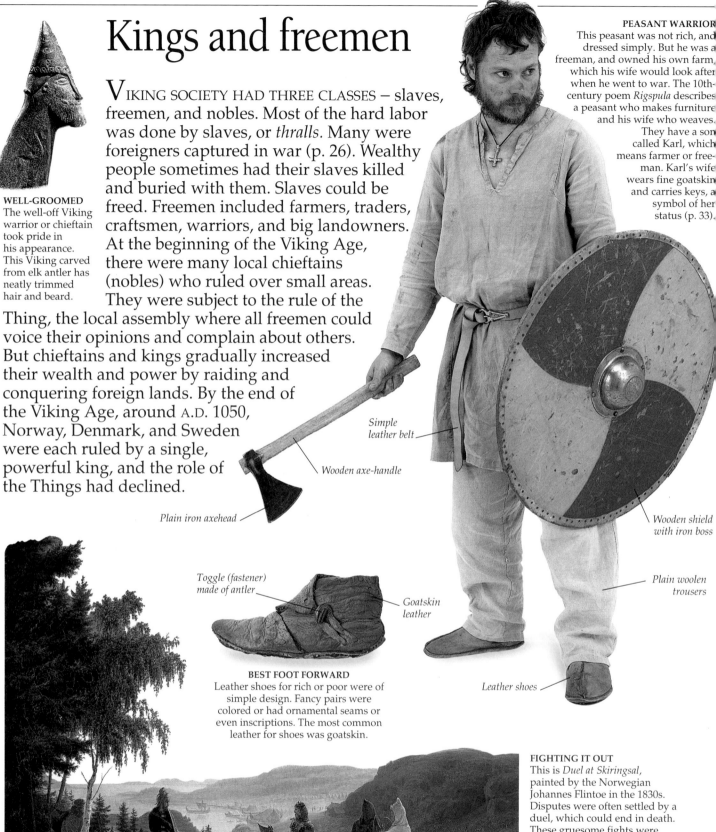

PEASANT WARRIOR
This peasant was not rich, and dressed simply. But he was a freeman, and owned his own farm, which his wife would look after when he went to war. The 10th-century poem *Rigspula* describes a peasant who makes furniture and his wife who weaves. They have a son called Karl, which means farmer or free-man. Karl's wife wears fine goatskin and carries keys, a symbol of her status (p. 33).

Simple leather belt

Wooden axe-handle

Plain iron axehead

Wooden shield with iron boss

Plain woolen trousers

Toggle (fastener) made of antler

Goatskin leather

Leather shoes

BEST FOOT FORWARD
Leather shoes for rich or poor were of simple design. Fancy pairs were colored or had ornamental seams or even inscriptions. The most common leather for shoes was goatskin.

FIGHTING IT OUT
This is *Duel at Skiringsal*, painted by the Norwegian Johannes Flintoe in the 1830s. Disputes were often settled by a duel, which could end in death. These gruesome fights were forbidden by law in Iceland and Norway around the year 1000. Arguments could also be sorted out by the Thing or by "ordeals." In these, men would try to prove their innocence by walking over red-hot iron or picking stones from a cauldron of burning water. The Vikings believed that the gods protected the innocent.

FANCY HAT
The rich wore expensive clothes and imported jewelry. These parts of an elaborate cap were made in Kiev in Ukraine and worn by a nobleman in Birka, Sweden.

Silver cap mount

Silver tassels

TO CAP IT OFF
This silk cap was worn by a rich man or woman in the Viking town of York, England. The silk may have been imported from faraway Constantinople.

Cloak embroidered with human faces

Bronze brooch for holding cloak in place

BROOCHES AND BUCKLES
All Viking men wore brooches and buckles to fasten their clothes. But the richer they were, the more ornate their brooch or buckle. These come from Gotland, Sweden.

Braids for fastening cloak

Wool tunic embroidered with animals and faces

Tunic was often worn over linen undershirt

Dyed woolen trousers

Bronze belt buckle

MAMMEN CHIEFTAIN
Fine clothes, tablecloths, white bread, and silver cups were all signs of nobility. This man is wearing a reconstruction of clothes found in a nobleman's grave in Mammen, Denmark. They are made of high-quality wool and silk, decorated with embroidered borders and even gold and silver thread. The noble couple in the poem *Rigspula* have a son called Iarl, which means earl. He owns land, rides horses, and can read and write runes (pp. 58–59). His wife Erna is slender and wise. Their youngest child is called Konr ungr, which means king.

Cloak of dyed wool with embroidered borders

BORDER FACES
The border of the Mammen cloak was a panel of imported silk embroidered with human faces. No one knows whose faces these are. But the beautiful decoration shows how wealthy the wearer was.

Fur trim

THINGS AND ALTHINGS
Each district had its own assembly, or Thing. Meetings were held outside at a special spot. This is a 19th-century painting of the Icelandic Althing, held once a year (p. 20). One observer said that "Icelanders have no king, only the law."

29

Women and children

VIKING WOMEN WERE INDEPENDENT. While the men were away on expeditions, women ran households and farms. A woman could choose her own husband, and could sue for divorce if he beat her or was unfaithful. On runestones (pp. 58–59), women were praised for their good housekeeping or skill in handiwork such as embroidery. Wealthy women raised runestones and paid for bridges to be built. Viking children had no school. Instead they worked in the fields and workshops, and helped with cooking, spinning, and weaving. Not all women and children stayed home. Many joined their husbands or fathers in colonies such as England. They hid somewhere safe during battles, and came out later to help set up new villages.

BRYNHILD
This is a romantic engraving of Brynhild. According to legend, she was a Valkyrie, a mythical woman warrior (p. 53). In reality, there is no evidence that any Viking women were warriors, or even traders or craftsworkers. But one female scald (poet) and a female rune carver are known.

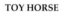

TOY HORSE
About 900 years ago, a small boy or girl in Trondheim, Norway, played with this toy horse made of wood. Children also had toy boats. They played board games and made music with small pipes (p. 50). In the summer young Vikings swam and played ball; in the winter they skated and played in the snow.

STARTING YOUNG
Viking boys played with toy weapons made of wood. They probably began serious weapon practice in their early teens. Some young men seem to have gone raiding when they were as young as sixteen.

Piece of leather covers point, so boys will not hurt each other

Toy spear made of wood

Woolen tunic with embroidered collar

Two carved animal heads with open jaws

Decorated belt tip

Toy sword

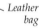

Leather bag

BONE SMOOTH
One of a woman's main responsibilities was making clothes for the whole family (pp. 44–45). After she had woven a piece of linen, a woman probably stretched it across a smoothing board and rubbed it with a glass ball until it was smooth and shiny. This board from Norway is made of whalebone.

Linen head-dress tied under the chin

Oval brooches

Child's tunic

Child's shoes

Over-dress

Long under-dress

Antler, probably from an elk

WELL COMBED
Combs carved out of bone or antler have been found all over the Viking world. These two are from Birka in Sweden. Viking men and women made sure their hair was well combed. They also used metal tweezers to pluck out unwanted hairs, and tiny metal ear scoops to clean out their ears.

Iron rivets

DAILY DRESS
Viking women were very particular about their appearance. This woman is wearing a long under-dress. On top she has a short over-dress, like a pinafore dress. This is held up by two oval brooches. An Arab who visited the town of Hedeby around A.D. 950 said that Viking women wore make-up around their eyes to increase their beauty. He also noted that many men did the same.

Hair tied in bun

Drinking horn

DRESS FASTENERS
Oval brooches were only worn by women. This pair comes from Ågerup in Denmark. Finding such brooches in a grave shows that the dead person was a woman. Although the cloth of the dress has usually rotted away, the position of the brooches on the shoulders shows how they were worn.

Train of dress

SWEDISH WOMAN
This silver pendant is from Birka, Sweden. It is in the shape of a woman in a dress with a triangular train. She is carrying a drinking horn, and may be a Valkyrie (p. 53).

Bead necklace

Knotted hairstyle

Large ring brooch

ALL DRESSED UP
Like the one above, this small pendant shows a well-dressed woman. She is wearing a shawl over a long, flowing dress. Her hair is tied in an elegant, knotted style. Her beads and a large brooch are easy to identify. The importance of pendants like these is unclear. They could have had some magical meaning. The figures represented may even be goddesses.

Shawl

Long under-dress with flowing train

Over-dress decorated with woven bands

31

At home

HOME LIFE REVOLVED around a central hall or living room. The layout was much the same all over the Viking world. A long, open hearth (fireplace) burned in the center, with a smoke hole in the ceiling above. The floor was stamped earth. The people sat and slept on raised platforms along the curved walls. Pillows and cushions stuffed with duck down or chicken feathers made this more comfortable. Well-off homes might have a few pieces of wooden furniture and a chest for precious belongings. Houses often had smaller rooms for cooking or spinning on either side of the main hall. Small buildings with low floors dug out of the ground were used as workshops, weaving sheds, animal barns, or houses for the poor. A chieftain's hall could be lined with wall hangings or carved or painted wooden panels. Around the year 1000, an Icelandic poet described panels decorated with scenes of gods and legends in the hall of a great chieftain. The poem was called *Húsdrápa*, which means "poem in praise of the house."

HOUSES, ICELANDIC STYLE
Good timber was scarce in Iceland and other North Atlantic islands (pp. 20–21). So houses usually had stone foundations, and walls and roofs made of turf. Some houses were dug into the ground, which kept them warm in winter and cool in summer. The walls were lined with wooden paneling to keep out the cold and damp.

Planks carved with beautiful animal heads

Slats join sideboards

SWEET DREAMS
Only the rich had chairs or beds. Ordinary Vikings sat on benches or stools or on the floor. At night, they stretched out on rugs on raised platforms. The wealthy woman in the Oseberg ship (pp. 54–57) was buried with not one, but three beds. This is a replica of the finest one. It is made of beech wood. The headboard planks are carved in the form of animal heads with arching necks (p. 9). The woman probably slept on a feather mattress, and was kept warm by a quilt filled with down or feathers.

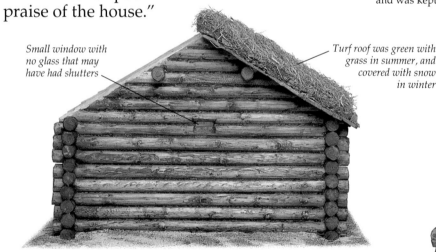

Small window with no glass that may have had shutters

Turf roof was green with grass in summer, and covered with snow in winter

End view of Trondheim house

Side view of Trondheim house

TRONDHEIM HOUSE
This is a model of a house built in Trondheim, Norway, in the year 1003. Its walls are horizontal logs notched and fitted together at the corners. A layer of birchbark was laid on the pointed roof and covered in turf. The bark would have kept the water out, while the earth and grass acted as insulation. Houses were built in various other ways, depending on local traditions and the materials at hand. Wooden walls were often made of upright posts, or staves, as in the Danish forts (pp. 22–23). Others had walls of wattle (interwoven branches) smeared with daub (clay or dung) to make them waterproof. Roofs could be covered in shingles (wooden tiles), thatch, turf, or matted reeds.

Loop to lift
hasp once lock
is opened

The key was put
in here

Curved hasp, part of
locking mechanism

SILVER FOR THE RICH
A rich Viking once drunk fruit wine
from this tiny silver cup. Only 1.7 in
(4.4 cm) high, it was found in Lejre
in Denmark. It is decorated
with four creatures with
human faces and
birdlike bodies.

Lock plate

Broken handle

The key was
turned and slid
to the bottom of
this slot to
unlock the box

Key for lock on left

Handle

Openwork
decoration,
including four
gripping beasts

LOCK UP
Women were
in charge of the
household, and especially the locked chest or box
where the family valuables were kept. This iron lock
comes from a box of maple wood. A woman in the 10th
century in Onsild, Jutland, Denmark, probably kept
coins or a few pieces of jewelry in it. When she died, she
was buried with the box and its key.

BRONZE KEY
A key was a symbol of
responsibility and dignity. This 9th-
century Danish key is made of beautifully
decorated cast bronze. Anyone who stole
from a locked chest was severely punished.

Roof rafters

Purlin, a pole that holds
up the main roof rafters

Door into main hall,
the house's only room

Thin layer of birchbark
keeps out rain

Thick layer of turf,
for insulation

Mealtime

ALL DAY LONG, the fire in the hearth was kept burning for cooking and heating. The hole in the roof above the fire didn't work very well, so Viking houses were always full of smoke. Rich households had baking ovens in separate rooms. These were heated by placing hot stones inside them. When darkness fell, work on the farm or in the workshop had to stop, and people would gather for the main meal of the day. The rich and the poor ate very different meals, served in different ways. For instance, most Vikings drank beer made from malted barley and hops. But while the poor drank from wooden mugs, the rich used drinking horns with fancy metal rims. They also enjoyed wine imported in barrels from Germany.

NORMAN FEAST
This feast scene from the Bayeux Tapestry (p. 10) shows a table laden with food and dishes. Wealthy Vikings had richly decorated knives and spoons and imported pottery cups and jugs. Ordinary people ate and drank from wooden bowls and cups.

FOOD FROM THE SEA
The sea was full of fish. For Vikings who lived near the coast, fish was the staple food. The bones of cod, herring, and haddock have been found in many Viking settlements. People also caught eels and freshwater fish, such as trout, in the many rivers and lakes that criss-cross Scandinavia.

HOME GROWN
Cabbages (above) and peas were most common vegetables. Man Vikings grew their own.

DRIED COD
Food had to be preserved so it would keep through the winter. Fish and meat were hung in the wind to dry. They could also be pickled in salt water. Salt was collected by boiling sea water, a boring job usually given to slaves. Fish and meat were probably also smoked.

Dried peas

Pine tree, source of kernels and bark

PEAS AND PINE BARK
Poor Vikings made bread with whatever they could find. One loaf found in Sweden contained dried peas and pine bark.

Cumin, a spice found in the Oseberg burial

FIT FOR A QUEEN
Horseradish was one of the seasonings found in the Oseberg burial (pp. 54–57), along with wheat, oats, and fruit.

A Norman cook lifts chunks of cooked meat off a stove with a two-pronged fork.

BAKING BREAD
Bread was kneaded in wooden troughs. Then it was baked on a griddle over a fire (as in this 16th-century Swedish picture) or in a pan that sat in the embers. Barley bread was most common, but rich people had loaves made of finer wheat flour.

POACHED EGGS
In the Atlantic islands, Viking settlers gathered gulls' eggs for eating. They also roasted the gulls.

GARLIC BULB
Like modern cooks, the Vikings added garlic and onion to meat stews and soups.

A HARE IN MY SOUP
Hares were trapped and hunted. The Vikings also hunted elk, deer, bears, wild boars, reindeer, seals, and whales for meat. Sheep, cattle, pigs, goats, geese, chickens, turkeys, and even horses were raised to be eaten.

Suspension loop

Iron handle

COOKING CAULDRON
Food was prepared around the hearth in the center of the living room. Meat was stewed in cauldrons, or huge pots, made of iron or soapstone. Some cauldrons were hung over the fire on a chain from the roof-beam. Others, like this one from the Oseberg ship, were suspended from a tripod.

CAUGHT ON THE WING
Game birds like this duck were trapped or hunted with short arrows. They would be roasted on a spit for a tasty meal.

One of the tripod's three legs

Raspberry

Blackberry

BERRY TASTY
Berries and wild fruits such as apples, cherries, and plums were gathered in the summer. Vikings may have grown fruit trees in gardens as well as picking fruit wild in the forest.

The pronged feet were stuck into the earth floor to keep the cauldron stable

Iron cauldron

Old crack   *Repair holes*

BAYEUX BARBECUE
In this scene from the Bayeux Tapestry (p. 10), two Norman cooks heat a cauldron. The fire sits in a tray like a barbecue. To the left, a third man lifts cooked chunks of meat off a stove onto a plate. The Vikings may have cooked in similar ways.

PATCHED
This clay cooking pot has four holes where a patch was stuck over a crack.

Animals, wild and imagined

BRONZE BEAST
This fierce animal with snarling teeth comes from a horse's harness bow (p. 43). It may have been made to scare enemies and protect the horse and wagon.

BROWN BEAR
Bears were hunted in the far north. Their skins were made into jackets and cloaks, and their claws and teeth were worn as pendants. Warriors may have thought that some of the bear's strength and courage would rub off on them (p. 14).

BEARS, WOLVES, mink, foxes, deer, and wild boar all roamed the dark forests of Norway and Sweden. Whales, otters, seals, walruses, and reindeer lived in the far north. Sea birds flocked along the coasts, and game birds were common inland. Viking legends are also stocked with these animals, most of which were hunted for their meat. They made clothes and bedding from the feathers, furs, and hides, and bones and tusks were raw materials for jewelry, tools, and everyday objects like knife handles. Many of the finest objects were then traded (pp. 26–27). But the animals that they decorated jewelry, tools, and weapons with are not real. Viking craftspeople imagined fantastic and acrobatic creatures. Animal hips become spirals, and plant shoots spring from their bodies. Some beasts become ribbons that twist around each other in intricate patterns.

STAG
Elk, deer, and reindeer all have big antlers. Craftsmen sawed and carved these to create combs (p.31). Deer skin was used for clothes and possibly wall and bed coverings. Venison (deer meat) was also dried, roasted, and eaten.

Head of animal

Bronze, cast in a mold

Gilt (gold-coated) silver

FANTASTIC ANIMAL
This brooch from Norway is in the shape of a slender, snake-like animal. It is caught up in a thin ribbon twisting in a fantastic pattern. This is known as the Urnes style of Viking art, after wood carvings on a church at Urnes in Norway.

Owl

Bird of prey

BIRD BROOCH
This brooch was found in a woman's grave in Birka, Sweden. It once decorated a belt worn by someone living in Eastern Europe by the river Volga (pp. 18–19). A Viking took it home to Sweden, where a jeweler converted it into a brooch. The birds are quite realistic, and the species are easy to identify. A Viking craftsman would have turned them into fantastic creatures.

GRIPPING BEAST
The acrobatic "gripping beast" became popular in Viking art in the 9th century. This playful animal writhes and turns inside out, gripping its own legs and even its throat.

Gripping beast from a 9th-century Danish brooch

Unlike deer, sheep do not shed their horns every year, so the horns get bigger with age

Each horn of an old Manx Loghtan ram can weigh 12 oz (350 g) and reach 1 ft 6 in (45 cm) in length

SNAKE CHARM
Snakes were common in Viking lands, and are important in poems and stories (p. 50–51). This silver snake pendant was worn by a Swedish woman as a good luck charm or amulet.

CAROLINGIAN CUP
Craftsmen in other areas based their decoration on real animals. This cup was made further south in the Carolingian Empire, in modern France or Germany. It is made of gilt (gold-coated) silver decorated with the figure of a bull-like animal and symmetrical leaves of the acanthus plant. The cup must have been traded or plundered, because it was found in a Viking hoard at Halton Moor, England, with a silver neck-ring (p. 47) and a gold pendant (p. 46).

LONE WOLF
The wolf roamed wild in the mountains of Scandinavia. Then, as now, people were terrified of its eerie howl. In the Viking myth of the end of the world, called *Ragnarök*, the god Odin is gobbled up by a monstrous wolf, Fenrir (p. 51). *Ragnarök* means the "Doom of the Gods."

HORNED HELMET
The Manx Loghtan sheep was a common farm animal in the Viking Age. Now it is only found on the Isle of Man, an island between England and Ireland that was colonized by Vikings in the 9th century. Sheep were kept all over the Viking world (pp. 40–41). In mountainous areas, Viking shepherds took their flocks to high pastures for the warm summer months. The Manx Loghtan sheep shed its wool naturally, so it didn't have to be sheared. It grew two, four, or sometimes even six horns.

37

Farming

MOST VIKINGS WERE FARMERS. They often had to work infertile land in harsh weather. The difficult conditions led many farmers to set sail for faraway lands like Iceland (pp. 20–21), where they hoped to find fertile soil and more space for their animals and crops. Sheep, cows, pigs, goats, horses, poultry, and geese were all raised for eating. The milk of cattle, goats, and sheep was drunk or turned into butter and cheese. Farms often had separate byres, sheds where cattle could pass the winter. Even so, many died of cold or starvation. Rich farms had byres to house a hundred cattle. A man's wealth was often measured in animals. Othere, a merchant from northern Norway, told King Alfred of England that he had 20 cattle, 20 sheep, 20 pigs, and a herd of 600 reindeer. But his main source of income was the furs he traded.

SHEARS
Vikings sheared sheep, cut cloth, and even trimmed beards with iron shears like these.

JARLSHOF FARM
The ruins of a 9th-century Viking farmhouse on the Shetland Islands. It had two rooms, a long hall and a kitchen. The farmers sat and slept on platforms that ran along the curved walls. A hearth burned in the center of the hall.

Thick fleece shed once a year, in spring

BLACK SHEEP
Hebridean sheep were farmed by Vikings on the Hebrides islands. Like Manx Loghtan sheep (p. 37), they shed their wool naturally, and do not have to be sheared. They can live on sparse vegetation and are very hardy.

Two sickle blades

Ard blade

MILKING REINDEER
This 16th-century Swedish engraving shows a woman milking reindeer. In the far north, people farmed reindeer for their milk, meat, and hides. They were also hunted in many places, including Greenland (pp. 20–21).

HARVEST TOOLS
The ground was broken up in the spring with an ard, a simple plow. Grain was cut with iron sickles with wooden handles. The blades of these tools were sharpened with whetstones (sharpening stones).

PLOWING AND SOWING
This detail from the Bayeux Tapestry (p. 10) shows Normans plowing (far left) and sowing seeds (left). The Vikings would have used similar techniques.

FLOUR POWER
Grain was ground into flour with a quern stone. This one comes from a Viking farm at Ribblehead in Yorkshire, England. The grain was placed on the bottom stone. Then the top stone was laid on it and the wooden handle was turned around. Rich Vikings preferred finer flour, ground with querns made of lava imported from the Rhineland in Germany.

Top stone

Bottom stone

Ears and grains of spelt wheat

GRAINS
Spelt is an early form of wheat. The Vikings also grew barley and rye.

Ground wheat

LONGHORN COW
Cattle like this were once farmed in many parts of the Viking world. Now that new breeds have been developed, longhorn cattle only survive on a few special farms. Domestic animals weren't just raised for their meat and milk. Sheep's wool, cattle hide, and poultry feathers were also used to make clothes and bedding. Cattle horns are hollow, and are ideal as drinking horns. These were tricky to put down, and had to be rested in special holders. Animal bones were carved into knife handles, combs, pins, needles, even jewelry.

Getting around

MUCH OF SCANDINAVIA is rugged and mountainous. The large forests, lakes, and marshes make traveling difficult, especially in bad weather. Vikings went by ship whenever possible. Traveling overland was often easiest in winter, when snow covered uneven ground and the many rivers and lakes froze over. People got around on sleighs, skis, and skates. In deep snow, they wore snow-shoes. Large sleighs were pulled by horses. To stop the horses from slipping on the ice, smiths nailed iron crampons, or studs, to their hooves. In the summer, Vikings rode, walked, or traveled in wagons pulled by horses or oxen. Roads were built on high land, to avoid difficult river crossings. The first bridge in Scandinavia, a huge wooden trestle, was built near Jelling in Denmark around the year 979, probably on orders from King Harald Bluetooth.

WELL GROOMED
A complete wooden wagon was found in the Oseberg burial ship (pp. 54–57). It is the only one known from Viking times. The surface is covered in carvings, including four heads of Viking men. The men all have well-groomed beards and mustaches.

A GOOD DEED
Christian Vikings thought building roads and bridges would help their souls go to heaven. This road in Täby, Sweden, was built by Jarlabanke (p. 59). He celebrated his good deed with a rune stone.

Bone ice skate from York, England

16th-century engraving of a Swedish couple skiing with single skis, as the Vikings did

ICE-LEGS
The word *ski* is Norwegian. Prehistoric rock carvings in Norway show that people have been skiing there for at least 5,000 years. The Vikings definitely used skis, though none have survived. Ice skates have been found all over the north. The Vikings called them "ice-legs." They were made by tying the leg bones of horses to the bottoms of leather boots. The skater pushed him or herself along with a pointed iron stick like a ski pole.

HORSING AROUND
Vikings were excellent riders. This silver horseman comes from Birka in Sweden, and dates from the 10th century. The rider is wearing a sword, and must be a warrior.

Beech body decorated in iron studs with tinned heads

One of four carved animal heads

Curved oak runners

SLEDGE
This is one of the three fine sledges from the Oseberg burial (pp. 54–57). The curved runners are carved with beautiful decorations. Lashed on top is an open box. Ferocious animal heads snarl from the four corners.

Copper alloy covered in gold

Hole through which reins passed

Ribbon decoration in Jellinge style

Animal heads, possibly meant to scare off evil spirits and stop horses from bolting

REINING THEM IN
Harness bows were only used in Denmark. The curved surface rested on a horse's back. The reins passed through the holes in the center to stop them from getting tangled up. This pair was found in a smith's hoard in Mammen, Jutland. They belonged to a wealthy chieftain, and were probably only used on ceremonial occasions. Their splendid decoration shows how wealthy he must have been.

Modern wood; original wood rotted away

Ornamental copper plates

Iron stirrups

Small gripping beast held in jaws of larger animal

DANISH STIRRUPS
Vikings were often buried with riding equipment such as stirrups, or even with their horses (pp. 54–57). These stirrups were found in a man's grave in Velds in Jutland, Denmark, along with horse bells, strap mounts, and a bit.

Silver eye

Side view

Front view

WELL TRAVELED
These stirrups are similar to the Danish pair. But they were found in the River Thames in London, and were probably made in England. Some Vikings took their riding equipment with them on their travels. They had to get horses from the local people, though.

41

In the workshop

THE VIKINGS PARTLY OWE THEIR SUCCESS to expert craftsmen who made their strong weapons and fast ships. The weapon-smith who forged sharp swords, spears, and axes (pp. 14–15) was the most respected. But the smiths who made the iron tools for working metal and wood were skilled, too. They knew how to work different metals and create elaborate decorations. Smiths also produced everyday objects like locks and keys, cauldrons for cooking, and iron rivets for ships. Highly trained Viking carpenters made a wide range of objects, including ships. They knew exactly what wood to use for what purpose, and how to cut timber to give maximum strength and flexibility. They could carve intricate designs and sometimes painted them with bright colors. Most of the colors have faded now, but enough paint survives to give an idea of the original effect.

Molding iron for making grooves or patterns on planks

PRESSED GOLD
This gold brooch from Hornelund in Denmark was made from a lead die. The jeweler pressed the die into a sheet of gold to create a pattern. Then he decorated the surface with gold wire and blobs or granules of gold. Only the richest chieftains or kings could afford such a beautiful brooch.

Twisted gold wire forms heart-shaped patterns

One of three heart-shaped loops made of strands of twisted gold wire

Plate shears for cutting sheet metal

Granules of gold

Plant decoration shows influences from western Europe, but the technique is purely Scandinavian

Lead die from Viborg, Denmark, used for making precious metal brooches like the Hornelund brooch

Smith's tongs for holding hot iron on anvil

MAKING DRAGONS
Bronze was heated in a crucible over a fire until it melted. Then the smith poured it into the stone mold. When the metal cooled, he lifted out a fine dragon head with a curly mane. It may have decorated a fancy box. A stone mold like this one could be used over and over again. Many brooches and dress pins (pp. 48–49) were cast in similar molds.

Modern casting

Stone mold for bronze dragon head from Birka, Sweden

Light hammerhead

Heavy hammer-head

HAMMERS
Hammers came in various weights. The heaviest were used for welding and forging swords, the lightest for delicate work like shaping wire.

Small detachable bit

Larger detachable bit, for boring bigger holes

AXES AND ADZES
The carpenter used an axe to fell (cut down) trees and chop off their branches. He then used a T-shaped axe (p. 15) to shape and smooth the planks. An adze has its blade at right angles to the handle. The carpenter could shape a log by chipping away at its surface with an adze.

Hole for wooden haft (handle)

Felling a tree with an axe

SHIP BUILDING
The Bayeux Tapestry (p. 10) shows how the Normans made ships. In the detail on the left, a man fells a tree. Above, a man trims a tree while another shapes the split trunks into planks with a T-shaped axe. Below, the planks are overlapped and riveted together. A carpenter smooths the planks. Another drills holes with a drill or auger, leaning against the curved end for extra force.

Adze head

SMITHING A SWORD
This carving is part of a 12th-century doorway from the church in Hylestad, Norway (p. 51). It shows the hero Sigurd breaking a sword the smith Regin has made for him. In another carving, Regin holds the hot iron with a pair of tongs and hits it with a hammer. A helper works the bellows to keep the fire in the forge burning.

Wood is modern, as original wood had rotted away

The carpenter turned this T-shaped handle to bore the hole

A BORING TOOL
This drill or auger was used to make holes in planks, including rivet holes that held ship planking together. It had five bits of different sizes.

A smith's tools
The tools on these two pages are part of a large hoard found in a chest at Mästermyr on the island of Gotland, Sweden. Their owner was a smith. He was able to work with sheet metal to make cauldrons and locks, but he could also cast, weld, and decorate bronze. He was a ship-builder, joiner, and wheelwright, and probably made the wooden tool chest as well!

Back gives extra strength

BONE CUTTER
A small hacksaw could cut through bone and metal. The carpenter could also use its narrow blade for fine work.

Tang, a spike that fits into a wooden handle

WOOD SAW
The small lengths of wood needed to make buckets, boxes, and furniture were cut with this large saw.

Iron toothed blade

Shaped end for carpenter to lean on

Wooden handle

Spinning and weaving

Viking women (and probably some men) spent part of the day spinning wool or flax. Then they wove the family's clothes on a vertical loom which stood against the wall. Everyday clothes were cut from plain wool. But the borders of men's tunics and women's dresses were woven with geometric patterns in bright colors or, for the very rich, gold and silver threads. Silk imported from far-off lands was made into hats and fancy borders for jackets. Fur trimmings on cloaks added a touch of style. Imitation fur was also fashionable.

Linen head cloth

Spindle whorl

SPINNING TOOLS
A spindle is a wooden rod used for spinning. It is passed through a spindle whorl, a round piece of clay or bone that makes the spindle spin with its weight. The weaver used rods called pin-beaters to straighten threads and make fine adjustments to the woven cloth.

Pin-beaters   Spindle

Wool being stretched and spun

Medieval woman spinning with raw wool held on a distaff

Raw wool

Brown silk

SPINNING A GOOD YARN
The spinner picks a tuft of raw wool from the basket and pulls it into a strand. She winds this around the spindle as it spins. When one tuft is spun, she adds the next tuft of wool to the strand.

Spun wool

Spindle whorl

Spindle

Raw, combed wool

FANCY CLOTHES
Fragments of a chieftain's clothes were found in a grave at Mammen, Denmark. They date from the late 10th century. This is the end of a long braid which the man may have used to fasten his cloak. It is made of silk, with gold embroidery on the borders. Animal figures and human faces also decorate the man's cloak and shirt. A reconstruction of his entire outfit can be seen on page 29. The beautiful Mammen Axe (pp. 6–7) was found in the same grave.

Cane basket

WEAVING ON A VERTICAL LOOM
The warp (vertical threads) on a vertical loom are kept taut by weights at the bottom. There are two sets of warp threads, one on each side of the beam. The weaver passes the weft (a horizontal thread) between the two. Then she raises the heddle rod, which brings the back warp to the front, and passes the weft back again. After each pass she uses a weaving batten to push the new weft against the cloth above. Pass by pass, the woven cloth grows longer .

Cross beam where finished cloth is rolled

Handle for turning beam as cloth is made

Wooden upright leaned against wall

Heddle rod with rest

Weft thread

Beam dividing the warp threads

Warp threads

Rest for beam

Finished cloth, made up of warp and weft threads

Hole for moving the position of the heddle-rod rest

Loom weights, heavy rings of clay or stone that keep the warp threads taut

45

Jewelry

GOLD PENDANT
Women wore pendants on the end of necklaces. This thin piece of embossed gold was worn as a pendant. It was found in a hoard (p. 49) in Halton Moor, England.

THE VIKINGS LOVED BRIGHT ornaments. Their metalworkers were highly skilled at the intricate decoration of jewelry. Both men and women wore brooches, necklaces, finger-rings, and arm-rings (like bracelets). Wearing gold and silver jewelry was a sign of wealth and prestige. After a successful raid, a king might reward a brave warrior by giving him a prize piece. Bronze didn't shine as brilliantly as gold, but it was less expensive. Pewter, a mixture of silver and other metals, was cheaper still. The poorest Vikings carved their own simple pins and fasteners from animal bones left over after cooking. Colored glass, jet, and amber were all made into pendants, beads, and finger-rings. Vikings also picked up fashions in jewelry from other countries and changed them to their own style.

Fine silver wires linked together as if they were knitted

SILVER ARM-RING
This massive arm-ring was found in Fyn in Denmark. It is solid silver, and must have weighed heavily on the arm. The surface is cut by deep, wavy grooves and punched with tiny rings and dotted lines. Four rows of beads decorate the center. They look as if they were added separately, but the whole piece was made in a mold (p. 42).

RECYCLING
Vikings who settled abroad took their fashions with them. This gold arm-ring was made in Ireland. Vikings raided many Irish monasteries in search of precious metals. Sacred books and objects often had mounts made of gold and silver, which they ripped out and carried away. Later, smiths would melt the metals down and turn them into jewelry.

Animal heads

Gold wires of different thicknesses coiled together

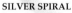

SILVER SPIRAL
Spiral arm-rings could be worn high on the upper arm. They were only popular in Denmark, and were imported from the Volga area of Russia. This fine silver ring was found near Vejle in Jutland, Denmark.

IN ALL HIS FINERY
This tough Viking is wearing every imaginable kind of jewelry. His bulging biceps are being squeezed by spiral arm-rings in the form of snakes. But in many details, the old drawing is pure fantasy (p. 6).

THOR'S HAMMER...
Thor's hammer (pp. 7, 53) was often worn as a pendant, just like the Christian cross. Here animal heads at the ends of the chain bite the ring from which the hammer hangs.

Grooves are filled with niello, a black compound, to make them stand out

...AND A CROSS
An open, leafy pattern decorates this silver Christian cross. The cross and chain were found in Bonderup, Denmark. They were probably made around the year 1050.

Four double-twisted gold rods braided together

Danish necklace made of glass beads

NECKLACES AND RINGS
The Arab traveler Ibn Fadhlan (pp. 19, 55) met Viking women in Russia around 920. He wrote that "round the neck they have ornaments of gold or silver." These would have included neck-rings, which are stiff and inflexible, and necklaces, which can twist and bend. This gold neck-ring is the largest and most splendid ever found. It is solid gold and weighs over 4 lb (1.8 kg). It could only have been worn by a broad-chested man, because it is more than 1 ft (30 cm) wide! Many Viking neck-rings were made by melting down silver Arab coins. Glass made the brightest beads. Bead-makers started with imported glass or broken drinking glasses. They heated these up and fused them together to make beads with bright patterns and swirling mixtures of colors.

Silver neck-ring from Halton Moor, England, made of braided silver wires

A farmer in Tissø in Denmark found this massive gold neck-ring while plowing a field

ARM-RING WITH TREES
This gold arm-ring from Råbylille in Denmark is stamped with some very fine decoration.

Tree

Cross

Gold ring from Denmark inscribed with runes (pp. 58–59)

Two gold finger-rings from Viking-age Ireland

THREE GOLD RINGS
Finger-rings were made like miniature arm-rings. Both men and women wore them. But Swedish women were the only ones to wear ear-rings, which they dangled from chains looped over the ear.

Continued on next page

Continued from previous page

Brooches

Clasps and brooches were often lavishly decorated. But they weren't just for show. All Vikings wore brooches to hold their clothes in place. Women usually had two oval brooches to fasten their overdresses (pp. 30–31). Men held their cloaks together with a single brooch on the right shoulder (pp. 28–29). In this way the right arm – the sword arm – was always free. Certain styles such as oval and trefoil brooches were popular all over the Viking world. Others, like the box brooches from Gotland, were only fashionable in certain areas.

Heads covered in gold — *Hair*

Beard — *Long mustache*

Ears

Tin-coated ring and pin

MEN'S HEADS
The tips of this brooch from Høm in Denmark are decorated with three men's heads. Each face has staring eyes, a neat beard, and a long mustache. Brooches like this were first made in the British Isles. The Vikings liked them so much they made their own.

One of four squatting human figures made of gold

Side view of bronze box brooch from Gotland

BOX BROOCH
Box brooches were shaped like drums. The magnificent brooch on the left comes from Mårtens on the island of Gotland, Sweden. A very wealthy woman wore it to fasten her cloak. The base is made of cast bronze, but the surface glitters with gold and silver.

Head of gripping beast

Top view of Mårtens box brooch, above

Head of slender animal

Front view   Back view

SHAPED LIKE CLOVER LEAVES
Trefoil brooches have three lobes. In the 9th and 10th centuries, women wore them to fasten their shawls. The finest ones were made of highly decorated gold and silver. Poorer women had simpler brooches, mass-produced in bronze or pewter. The trefoil style was borrowed from the Carolingian Empire to the south of Scandinavia, in what is now France and Germany.

GRIPPING BEASTS
Four gripping beasts (p. 39) writhe across this silver brooch made in Hunderup in Denmark. It was found at the site of Nonnebakken, one of the great Viking forts (pp. 22–23).

URNES AGAIN
The Urnes art style featured a snaky animal twisting and turning in dynamic coils (p. 38) It was the most popular decoration for 11th-century brooches, like this bronze one from Roskilde, Denmark.

THE PITNEY BROOCH
The Urnes art style was very popular in England and Ireland during the reign of Cnut the Great (1016–35). This beautiful gold brooch in the Urnes style was found at Pitney in Somerset, England.

Long pin would have been stuck through cloak

Bronze pin, possibly from a brooch, in Irish style but found in Norway

BURIED TREASURE
The silver objects at the top of this page are all from a hoard found in Goldsborough churchyard in Yorkshire, England. The big "thistle" brooch was probably made in England. Buried with it were fragments of brooches and arm-rings, and another brooch without its pin.

Animal head

Silver brooch with missing pin

Silver thistle brooch

Bosses (knobs) like thistles that give brooch its name

Pieces of hack silver

Hack silver

Cut coin

Silver with a thin coating of gold

Boss broken off of a thistle brooch

Hoards

There were no banks in Viking times. So many Vikings buried their valuables in a secret spot for safe-keeping. These stashes of buried treasure are called hoards. If a Viking died in battle or just forgot where a hoard was hidden, it could lie in the ground for centuries. Over a thousand Viking hoards have been found. The largest one, found in Cuerdale, England, contained 88 lb (40 kg) of silver. Hoards may include jewelry, coins, gold and silver ingots, and hack silver – pieces of chopped-up silver, coins, or jewelry (p. 27).

Amber set in head of pin

Piece of inlaid blue glass

IRISH BROOCH IN A NORWEGIAN GRAVE
What was this Irish brooch doing in a woman's grave in Norway? She was buried in the 10th century, but the brooch was made at least a hundred years earlier in Ireland. Her husband may have bought or stolen it on an expedition to Ireland.

Round end decorated in gold with animal forms

Silver ring and pin inlaid with gold

WEIGHED DOWN BY FASHION
One of the biggest pieces of Viking jewelry known, this silver brooch was found at Møllerløkken on the Danish island of Fyn. It is called a penannular brooch. It was made in Scandinavia, but the style was based on dress pins the Vikings saw in the British Isles. Huge brooches with pins this long must have been cumbersome and dangerous to wear. Their main purpose was to show off the owner's wealth. An Icelandic story tells of a poet who wrote a wonderful patriotic poem. As a reward he was given a silver brooch that weighed 25 lb (11.5 kg) – 32 times more than this one! The delighted poet sold the monster brooch and bought a farm.

Interlace decoration engraved and inlaid with the black compound niello

Games, music, and stories

A FEAST WAS A TIME to relax. After they had eaten their full, Vikings played games, told stories, and listened to music. Kings had their own poets, called scalds, who entertained guests and praised the king. Stories and poems were told from memory and passed down from father to son. People knew all the exciting episodes by heart. Popular legends like Thor's fishing trip were carved on stone or wood (p. 58–59). Jesters and jugglers often amused the guests with tricks and funny dances. Some games were played on elaborate boards with beautifully carved pieces. Others were scratched on wood or stone. Broken pieces of pottery or scraps of bone could be used as counters. Many outdoor pastimes were the same as today. During the long winters, Vikings went skiing, sledging, and skating (p. 40). In the summer, they fished, swam, and went boating in the cold rivers and fjords.

HORSE FIGHTING
These Icelandic ponies are fighting in the wild. Vikings enjoyed setting up fights between prize stallions (male horses). It was a serious matter, with bets laid on the winner. Horse-fighting may have played a part in religious feasts and ceremonies. The Vikings may have thought the winning horse was a special favorite of the gods.

SWEET HARP
In rich households, musicians played the harp or lyre to accompany stories and poems. Vikings were also keen singers. Talented singers would perform at feasts, and the whole assembly might join in a ballad or a popular folk song.

Such a headdress may have started the myth about Vikings wearing horned helmets

Blow here

Sound is produced as air passes this hole

BONE FLUTE
A Swedish Viking made this flute by cutting holes in a sheep's leg bone. He or she played it like a recorder, by blowing through one end. Covering the finger holes produced different notes.

Carved human head

Carved border decoration in Borre art style

Stave

Sword

Fingers cover bottom holes

Game pieces fit into 49 holes in board

BALLINDERRY BOARD
A popular Viking board game was *hneftafl*. One player used his eight pieces to protect the king from the other player, who had 16 pieces. This wooden board from Ballinderry, Ireland may have been used for *hneftafl*. The central hole could have held the king.

DANCING GOD
This silver figure from Sweden may be a "dancing god." He is carrying a sword in one hand and a stave or spear in the other. Dancing was popular after feasts, and played a part in religious ceremonies. Some dances were slow and graceful. In the wilder ones, the dancers leapt about violently. After the coming of Christianity (pp. 62–63), priests tried to stop dancing altogether.

FIGURES OF FUN
Gaming pieces could be simple counters or little human figures. This amber man (far right) may have been the king in a game of *hneftafl*. He is holding his beard in both hands.

Two walrus ivory gaming pieces from Greenland

Amber gaming piece from Roholte, Denmark

Hands hold beard

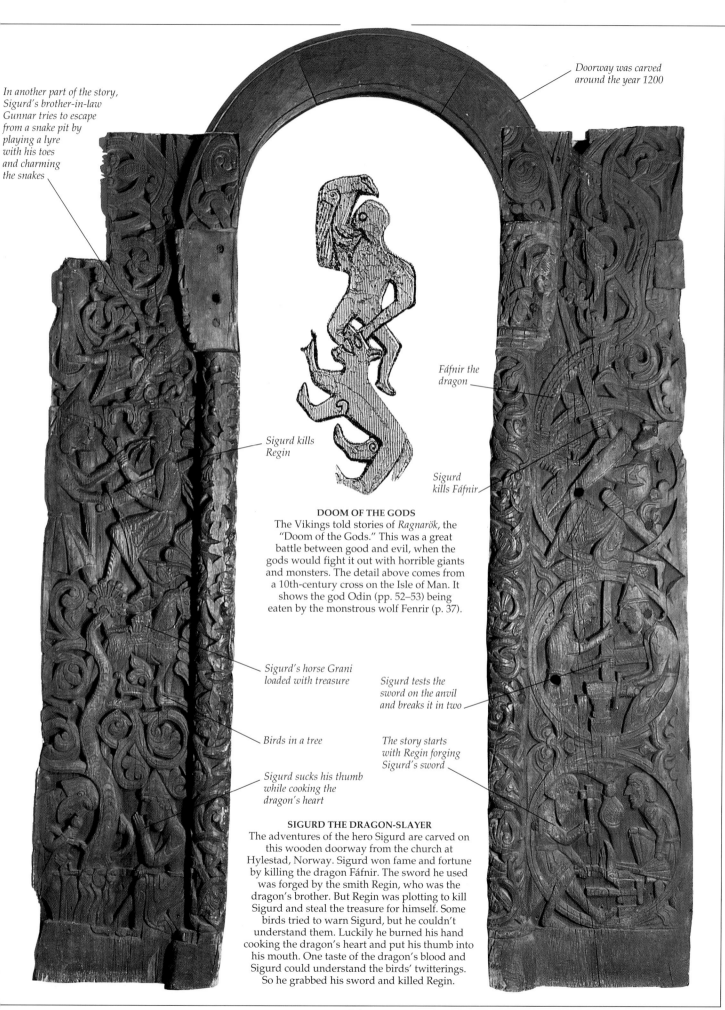

In another part of the story, Sigurd's brother-in-law Gunnar tries to escape from a snake pit by playing a lyre with his toes and charming the snakes

Doorway was carved around the year 1200

Sigurd kills Regin

Fáfnir the dragon

Sigurd kills Fáfnir

DOOM OF THE GODS

The Vikings told stories of *Ragnarök*, the "Doom of the Gods." This was a great battle between good and evil, when the gods would fight it out with horrible giants and monsters. The detail above comes from a 10th-century cross on the Isle of Man. It shows the god Odin (pp. 52–53) being eaten by the monstrous wolf Fenrir (p. 37).

Sigurd's horse Grani loaded with treasure

Sigurd tests the sword on the anvil and breaks it in two

Birds in a tree

The story starts with Regin forging Sigurd's sword

Sigurd sucks his thumb while cooking the dragon's heart

SIGURD THE DRAGON-SLAYER

The adventures of the hero Sigurd are carved on this wooden doorway from the church at Hylestad, Norway. Sigurd won fame and fortune by killing the dragon Fáfnir. The sword he used was forged by the smith Regin, who was the dragon's brother. But Regin was plotting to kill Sigurd and steal the treasure for himself. Some birds tried to warn Sigurd, but he couldn't understand them. Luckily he burned his hand cooking the dragon's heart and put his thumb into his mouth. One taste of the dragon's blood and Sigurd could understand the birds' twitterings. So he grabbed his sword and killed Regin.

51

Gods and legends

THE VIKINGS BELIEVED IN MANY different gods and goddesses. The gods all had their own personalities, rather like human beings. The chief gods were Odin, Thor, and Frey. Odin, the god of wisdom and war, had many strange supernatural powers. Thor was more down-to-earth. He was incredibly strong, but he wasn't very clever. Frey, a god of fertility, was generous. The German traveler Adam of Bremen visited Uppsala in Sweden in 1075. He saw a great temple with statues of Odin, Thor, and Frey. Earlier in the Viking Age, people worshipped outdoors, in woods or mountains or by springs or waterfalls.

Cone-shaped hat

One hand holding beard, a symbol of growth

THREE GODS?
These three figures have been identified as Odin (left) Thor (middle), and Frey (right). But they may be kings or Christian saints. They are on a 12th-century tapestry from Skog church in Sweden (p. 63).

GODLY FAMILY
Frey was a god of fertility and birth. The best image of him is this small statue from Södermanland in Sweden. It is only 2.8 in (7 cm) high. People called on Frey in the spring for rich crops. When they got married, they asked Frey to bless them and give them many children. His sister Freyja was a goddess of fertility and love. One story says that half the warriors killed in battle went to join Freyja, while the rest went to Odin.

MONSTROUS MASK
Frightening faces were sometimes drawn on memorial stones or pieces of jewelry (p. 7). They may be gods, or they might have been meant to scare off evil spirits. This face from a stone in Århus, Denmark, has a long braided beard and glaring eyes.

HIS LIPS ARE SEALED
Loki was part god and part devil. He could change his shape, and was always getting into mischief. In one story, Loki made a bet with a dwarf that he was a better metalworker. While the dwarf was heating up the furnace with bellows, Loki tried to distract him by turning into a fly and stinging him. But the dwarf won the bet anyway. To punish Loki and keep him quiet, he sewed his lips together. This stone bellows-shield shows Loki with his lips sewn up.

Silver Thor's hammer from Denmark

THOR'S HAMMER
Thor was popular with peasants and farmers. He rode through the sky in a chariot pulled by goats. There are many stories of his battles against evil giants and monsters, which he clubbed to death with his mighty hammer (p. 7).

A HERO'S WELCOME
The Valkyries were warrior women who searched battle-fields for dead heroes. They carried warriors who had died bravely to Valhalla, the Viking heaven. Here Odin welcomed the dead heroes, joining them in feasts in the great hall every evening.

A GIANT TAKES A BRIDE
In one story, the giant Thrym stole Thor's hammer. He said he would only give it back if he could marry Freyja. So Thor dressed up as Freyja and went to the ceremony. He nearly gave himself away by drinking too much! When Thrym brought out the hammer to bless the bride, Thor grabbed it and killed him and all the giant guests.

Dead warrior

Curved roof of Valhalla

Valkyrie (left) and man with axe (right)

Valkyrie with drinking horn greets dead hero

Runic inscription

Sail and rigging

PICTURES OF VALHALLA
A hero arrives in Valhalla on this picture stone from Gotland (p. 58). He is riding Odin's eight-legged horse, Sleipnir. A Valkyrie holds up a drinking horn to welcome him. Under the curved roof of Valhalla, another Valkyrie gives a drinking horn to a man with an axe and a dog.

Hero riding the eight-legged horse Sleipnir arrives in Valhalla

WATERFALL OF THE GODS
In Iceland, gods were worshipped at Godafoss, which means "waterfall of the gods."

TEARS OF GOLD
Freyja married a god called Od, who left her. All the tears she wept for him turned to gold. In this romantic picture, she is searching the sky for him in a chariot pulled by cats.

Ship full of armed warriors

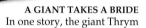

Viking burials

BEFORE THE COMING of Christianity, Vikings were buried with everything they thought they would need in the afterworld. Funeral ceremonies varied a lot, and much is still shrouded in mystery. The wealthiest men and women were buried in ships, to carry them to the next world. These were crammed full of their belongings, from clothes and weapons to kitchen goods and furniture. Horses, dogs, even servants were killed and laid to rest with the dead Viking. The ships were then covered with mounds of earth, or set alight in a blazing funeral pyre. There are stories about burning ships being pushed out to sea, although there is no proof that this ever really happened. Other Vikings were placed in underground chambers in burial mounds. Even poor peasants were buried with their favorite sword or brooch.

Prow ends in snake's head

Intricate carvings of lively animals

BAGGY TROUSERS
Three acrobatic human figures are carved inside the prow of the Oseberg ship. They have long, wispy beards and are doing strange gymnastics in baggy trousers.

BURIAL MOUND
Amazing riches have been dug out of some burial mounds. Entire ships have survived in the right soil conditions. Even when the wood has disintegrated, the ship's outlines may be left in the earth. A ship from a mound in Ladby on Fyn, Denmark, has been traced in this way. Many mounds contain burial chambers, not ships.

Strakes get narrower toward the prow

Twelve strakes, each overlapping the one below

Stem is a single piece of fine oak, joined to keel at base

THE OSEBERG SHIP
The most beautiful Viking ship of all is the Oseberg ship. It was discovered in 1903 in a burial mound in Oseberg near the Oslo Fjord in Norway. Like the Gokstad ship (pp. 8–9), it had been preserved by the soggy blue clay of the fjord, or inlet. This is a modern copy of the fine oak prow. Only fragments of the original were left in the mound. Like the sternpost, the prow is carved with a brilliant array of animals and people. It ends in a curling snake's head, and the tip of the stern is the snake's tail. The ship is 70 ft 6 in (21.5 m) long and has 15 oar-ports (holes) on each side. As many as 30 men were needed to row it. But the Oseberg ship is a frail vessel that couldn't have sailed the open ocean. It was probably only used for state occasions or sailing up and down the coast. A mass of ship's equipment, including a gangplank, bailing bucket, mast, rudder, steering oar, anchor, and 15 pairs of oars, was found inside.

REBUILDING THE OSEBERG SHIP

The Oseberg burial mound was 144 ft (44 m) long and 20 ft (6 m) high. It was excavated in the summer of 1904. The ship inside was in bad condition. It had been filled with heavy stones, which had broken the wood into thousands of fragments. Each fragment was numbered, washed, and protected with preservatives. Then the ship was put back together, piece by piece.

INSIDE THE BURIAL SHIP

The Oseberg ship is the most sumptuous relic of a Viking burial. The bones of two women were found inside. They had been buried in the mid 9th century. Judging by the rich furnishings, one was probably a queen. The other may have been her slave or servant. The dead women must have once lain on the beds found in the burial chamber. These were littered with down and other remains of bedding. Two oxen and at least 10 horses had been slaughtered and thrown into the ship. Inside as well were a richly carved wooden wagon, three beautiful sleighs (p. 40), a work-sleigh, and many pieces of furniture, tapestries, and kitchenware such as an iron cooking cauldron (p. 35). The carving on some of these objects is superb.

Prow, a snake's head in a spiral

Mast

Sternpost

Bailing bucket

Pine shield rack

Oars

Oar-ports

Hull of ship is made of oak

Keel, nearly 65 ft 8 in (20 m) long, made of two pieces of oak

WE BURN HIM IN A MOMENT

This is a re-enactment of a Viking funeral pyre. The Arab chronicler Ibn Fadhlan (pp. 19, 47) saw a Viking chieftain's funeral in Russia in 922. The dead man was dressed in beautiful clothes and seated in the ship, surrounded by drinks, food, and weapons. Then various animals and finally a woman were killed and laid in the ship with him. Then the ship was set on fire. Ibn Fadhlan was told: "We burn him in a moment and he goes at once to paradise."

BURIED BROOCH

No jewelry was found in the Oseberg ship, because the mound had been robbed long ago. But this bronze brooch was found in a woman's grave nearby. It is in the shape of an exotic animal with an arched head. The style is very similar to some of the Oseberg wood carvings.

BURIAL CHEST

The burial chamber of the Oseberg ship contained the fragments of many wooden chests. This is the most well preserved one. It is made of oak wood decorated with broad iron bands. The elaborate locking system includes three iron rods that end in animal heads. The chest was full of tools, which the dead woman may have needed to repair her vehicles in the next world.

Rows of nails decorate and secure the iron bands

One of three rods with animal heads

Continued on next page

Buried treasure

Vikings were buried with all kinds of treasures.
These are known as grave goods. They are usually
the finest or favorite belongings the dead man or
woman owned or wore. Other grave goods were
specially made, just to be buried. Grave goods give
many glimpses of Viking life, of how people cooked
or sewed, of their furniture, dress, and jewelry,
and of the tools and weapons
they used every day.

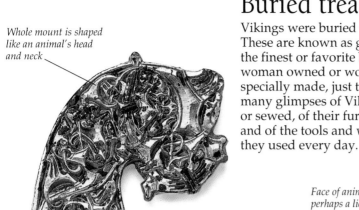

*Whole mount is shaped
like an animal's head
and neck*

Head of person or animal

Paw

*Tangle
of legs*

*Two animal heads in profile,
staring snout to snout*

*Face of animal,
perhaps a lion*

Eye

Long neck

*Slender,
S-shaped
animal*

*Back
leg*

Front leg

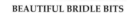

Bird

BEAUTIFUL BRIDLE BITS
These five glittering pieces are part of a
horse's bridle from the late 8th century. They were
found with 17 others in a rich man's grave in Broa in
Gotland, Sweden. Made of bronze and coated with
gold, they are decorated with masses of intricate
animals and birds, some twisting in slender
ribbons, others plump and gripping everything
in sight (p. 37).

Cast bronze handle

*Spiral patterns
engraved on
bronze sheets*

DRINKS BUCKET
Made in northern
England or Scotland,
this bucket was
buried in a woman's
grave in Birka,
Sweden, around 900.
It is made of birch
wood covered in
sheets of bronze.
The bucket was
probably used for
serving drinks.

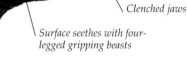

Fang

Clenched jaws

*Surface seethes with four-
legged gripping beasts*

The so-called "Carolingian"
animal-head post

Mysterious heads

Among the treasures in the
Oseberg ship-burial were five
strange wooden posts. Here are
three of them. Each post is
carved in a different style, but
they are all topped by fantastic
creatures with snarling mouths.
The carvers were incredibly
skilled. The animals' heads and
necks squirm with a mass of
tiny figures. No one knows what
the posts were for. Worshippers
might have carried them at a
religious procession, perhaps at
the Oseberg funeral. The fierce
animals, like lions, may have
been meant to scare off
evil spirits.

THE ENGLISH WAY
In their homes in Scandinavia, the Vikings raised huge memorial stones to remember dead friends or relatives (pp. 58–59). These stood in public places, often far from the dead person's grave. But in their colonies in England, the Vikings adopted the native custom of gravestones. This fragment of a stone from Newgate is decorated with two animals, one devouring the other. Traces of red paint show that it was once brightly colored.

Head of first animal

Second animal swallowing the first

PLANTS AND ANIMALS
These twisting figures decorate an 11th-century English gravestone. Two animals with S-shaped bodies form a figure eight pattern. Plant leaves and shoots sprout from their snaking bodies.

SHIPS IN STONE
Only the very rich could afford a real ship to carry them to the next world. Other Vikings had their graves marked with raised stones in the shape of a ship. These ship settings are common all over Scandinavia. This is one of a whole fleet of ships in the big graveyard at Lindholm Høje in Jutland, Denmark.

Flaring nostrils

Swirling circles carved in very high relief

Large glaring eyes

Metallic fangs and eyes

Surface decorated with hundreds of nails with heads shaped like flowers

Open jaw with large bared teeth

Two elegant, intertwining animals

The "First Baroque" animal-head post

The "Academician's" animal-head post

All five posts had long wooden planks attached to their bases with wooden dowels, or pins

VIKING SOAP OPERA
This romantic painting shows the funeral pyre of Sigurd the dragon-killer (pp. 51, 58) and Brynhild (p. 30). In the legend, Sigurd was in love with Brynhild. But he married another woman instead and tried to trick Brynhild into marrying his brother-in-law, Gunnar. Brynhild was so angry that she had Sigurd killed. Overcome with grief, she stabbed herself and joined Sigurd on his funeral pyre.

Runes and picture stones

VIKINGS CELEBRATED BRAVERY in battle and the glory of dead relatives by raising memorial stones. These were carved with pictures and writing in runic letters (runes), often inside an intricate border of snakes. Some stones were raised by people who wanted to show off their own achievements. Others tell of loved ones who died on far-off voyages. The stones were set up in public places where many people could stop and admire them. The unusual picture stones from the island of Gotland often have no runes. But they are crowded with lively scenes of gods, ships, and warriors.

Sigurd's horse

Birds

Sigurd sucks his thumb

Dragon Fáfnir

Headless body of Regin

Sigurd kills dragon

SIGURD THE DRAGON KILLER
The complete legend of Sigurd (p. 51) is carved on a great rock at Ramsund in Sweden. The carver has cleverly fitted clues about all the episodes into the frame made of snakes. He has also turned one of the serpents into the dragon Fáfnir.

Warrior killed in battle

The eight-legged horse Sleipnir carries Odin through the sky

The large piece of limestone was carved and painted in the 8th century

Interlace border

Headless bodies of the king's two sons

Völund's forge with his hammer and tongs

Wild beast, perhaps a wolverine

A JUMBLE OF PICTURES
This picture stone from Ardre, Gotland, is a jumble of pictures. But several stories can be picked out. At the top, Odin's mysterious eight-legged horse, Sleipnir, carries the god across the sky. Below is a Viking ship, surrounded by episodes from the bloody story of Völund the blacksmith. He was taken prisoner by King Nidud. In revenge, Völund cut off the heads of both of the king's sons and made their skulls into cups. In the end, Völund escaped by forging a pair of wings and flying away. The small boat below the ship may be the god Thor fishing with the giant Hymir. According to the legend, Thor caught the World Serpent. But Hymir was so terrified that he cut the line.

Ship full of warriors, with large rectangular sail

May be Thor and Hymir fishing from small boat

The bird may be Völund flying away

Two figures fishing

Many other pictures cannot be identified with certainty

Medieval calendar stave carved with 657 different symbols

Writing in runes

Runes were easy to carve in stone or wood, with straight or diagonal lines. The basic alphabet had 16 runes. Runes were still used in Scandinavia well into the Middle Ages. The calendar stave (staff) from Sweden (above) shows how they developed.

Snake's tail

Runic text inside snakes

INSCRIBED ANTLER
Bills, accounts, even love messages were written in runes on sticks. Part of this deer's antler from Dublin, Ireland, has been flattened to make a space for an inscription.

Runes begin: "Hart's horn…"

Secret runes which have not been deciphered

SECRET RUNES FROM GREENLAND
This pine stick from c. 1000 has the runic alphabet on one side. The other two sides are carved with secret and magical runes. No one knows what they mean.

Cross, which shows that Jarlabanke was a Christian

Snake's head

THORFAST'S COMB
Everyday objects were sometimes labeled in runes to declare their owner or maker. The runes on this comb case say: "Thorfast made a good comb."

F U TH A R K H N I A S T B M L R

FUTHARK
The basic runic alphabet was called *futhark*, after the first six letters. The first runic inscriptions, from around A.D. 200, are in a longer alphabet, with 24 characters. Around the year 800, the Viking alphabet with eight fewer runes was developed. Most inscriptions on stone were in normal runes. Another version of the alphabet was used for everyday messages on wood or bone.

SHOWING OFF
Jarlabanke was a wealthy 11th-century landowner who thought a lot of himself. He built a road over marshy land at Täby in Sweden. Then he raised four rune stones, two at each end, to remind travelers of his good deed. He also had this stone erected in the churchyard of Vallentuna, a village nearby. The runes say: "Jarlabanke had this stone raised in memory of himself in his lifetime, and made this Thing place, and alone owned the whole of this Hundred." The "Thing place" was the spot where the assembly for the district met (pp. 28–29). A Hundred was the area governed by a Thing.

SAINT PAUL'S STONE
In 1852, the end slab of a splendid tomb was found in the churchyard of St. Paul's Cathedral in London, England. The whole tomb must have been shaped like a box. This is a color painting of the great beast (p. 56) that decorates the slab. The colors are based on tiny traces of pigment found on the stone. The beast is very dynamic, twisting and turning around a smaller animal. The decoration shows that it was carved in the 11th century. The runes on the edge of the slab say: "Ginna and Toki had this stone set up." These two may have been warriors in Cnut the Great's army. Cnut became King of England in 1016 (p. 63).

The Jelling Stone

THE GREATEST STONE MONUMENT in Scandinavia is the Jelling Stone. It was raised by King Harald Bluetooth at the royal burial place of Jelling in Jutland, Denmark. Beside the stone are two huge mounds. One of these, the North Mound, may be where Harald's parents, King Gorm and Queen Thyre, were buried in a traditional ceremony (pp. 56–57). When Harald became a Christian, he built a church next to the mounds and had his parents re-buried inside. Then he raised the Jelling Stone in their memory. The memorial also advertised his own power as king of Norway and Denmark. This a modern copy of the stone. It is a three-sided pyramid, with a long inscription on one side and pictures on the other two.

SILVER MOUNT
King Gorm may have worn this mount on his belt. It was found in a grave in the church in Jelling, among the reburied bones of a man, probably Gorm.

Two entwined ribbon-like animals

GORM'S CUP?
This silver cup, usually known as the Jelling Cup, was found in the North Mound. It is the size of an egg. King Gorm may have drunk fruit wine from it. The cup is decorated with ribbon-like animals that gave their name to a style of Viking art, the Jellinge style.

Original stone is a single, massive boulder of red-veined granite

The great beast, a wild animal with sharp claws and a long tail

The beast is entwined in the coils of a huge snake

Ribbon-like decoration in the Mammen style, a development of the Jellinge style seen on the cup, with the ribbons based on plants rather than animals

Runes here continue from the inscription on the first side, reading: "…and Norway…"

GREAT BEAST
One side of the stone is carved with a snake twisting and turning around a great animal. Their struggle may represent the battle between good and evil. The animal could be a lion, but it is often just called "the great beast." It became a popular image in Viking art, and can be seen on weather vanes (p. 9) and rune stones like the St. Paul's Stone (p. 59).

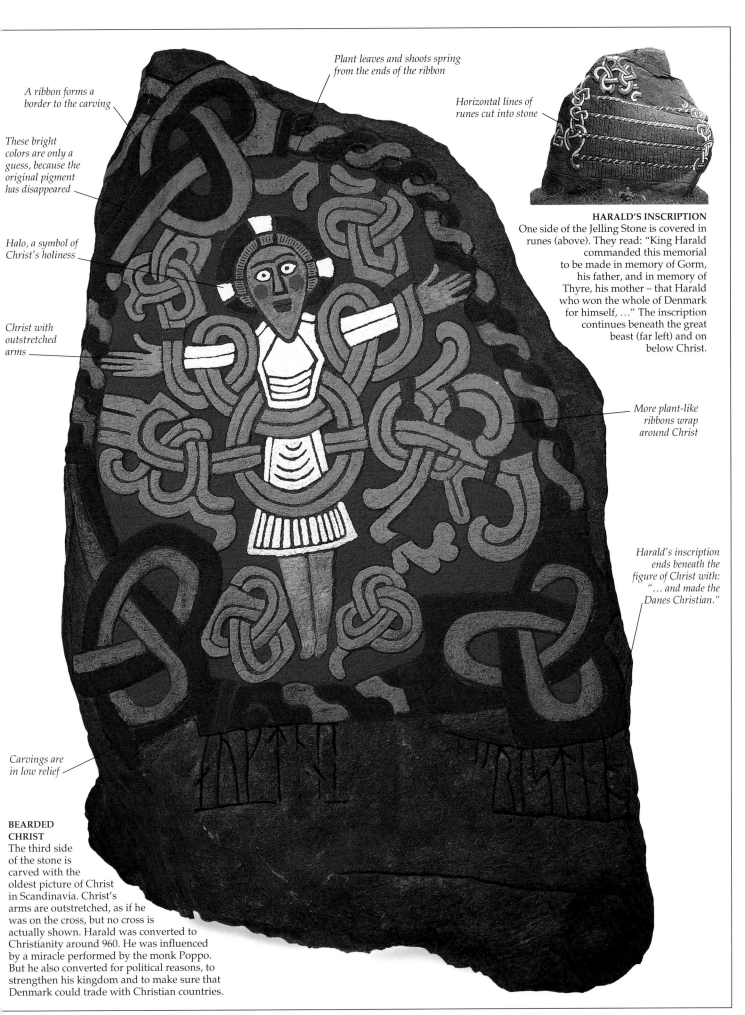

Plant leaves and shoots spring
from the ends of the ribbon

A ribbon forms a
border to the carving

These bright
colors are only a
guess, because the
original pigment
has disappeared

Halo, a symbol of
Christ's holiness

Christ with
outstretched
arms

Horizontal lines of
runes cut into stone

HARALD'S INSCRIPTION
One side of the Jelling Stone is covered in
runes (above). They read: "King Harald
commanded this memorial
to be made in memory of Gorm,
his father, and in memory of
Thyre, his mother – that Harald
who won the whole of Denmark
for himself, …" The inscription
continues beneath the great
beast (far left) and on
below Christ.

More plant-like
ribbons wrap
around Christ

Harald's inscription
ends beneath the
figure of Christ with:
"… and made the
Danes Christian."

Carvings are
in low relief

**BEARDED
CHRIST**
The third side
of the stone is
carved with the
oldest picture of Christ
in Scandinavia. Christ's
arms are outstretched, as if he
was on the cross, but no cross is
actually shown. Harald was converted to
Christianity around 960. He was influenced
by a miracle performed by the monk Poppo.
But he also converted for political reasons, to
strengthen his kingdom and to make sure that
Denmark could trade with Christian countries.

The coming of Christianity

SCANDINAVIA WAS SURROUNDED by Christian countries. Viking traders often wore crosses so they could travel freely through Christian lands (p. 27). But most Vikings remained loyal to the old gods until late in the 10th century. Then kings started supporting missionaries from England and Germany because they saw Christianity as a way to strengthen their power. Denmark converted to Christianity in the 960s, under King Harald Bluetooth. Norway followed early in the 11th century. In Sweden, the traditional beliefs survived until the end of the 11th century (p. 52). The Vikings finally gave the old gods up when they saw that kings or missionaries who destroyed their statues were not punished by Odin, Thor, or Frey.

RESURRECTION EGG
This colorful egg was a symbol of Christ's resurrection. It was made in Russia, and may have been brought to Sweden by Russian missionaries.

THE CHURCH AND THE SWORD
King Olaf Haraldsson turned Norway into a Christian country around 1024. He had old temples destroyed and forced people to convert.

STAVE CHURCH
Wooden churches were put up all over Scandinavia as soon as the people converted to Christianity. They were built like Viking houses, with wooden staves (planks) set upright in the ground. The first stave churches were simple, one-story buildings. By the 12th and 13th centuries, elaborate churches with many roofs were being built. This is the stave church from Gol in Norway, built around 1200, and now in the Folk Museum in Oslo.

Spire

Turret

Gables decorated with carved dragon heads like ones on reliquary, or shrine

More carved dragons

Portals are all crowned with crosses

LIKE A LITTLE CHURCH
Just like a miniature church, this little shrine or reliquary is decorated with dragon heads. Reliquaries were built to hold holy Christian relics. This one was made for Eriksberg church on Gotland, Sweden, in the late 1100s. Four little animal paws hold it up. The reliquary glitters with a thin layer of gold over its frame of carved wood. It probably once held bones or fragments of cloth that people believed came from the body or clothes of a saint.

Roofed-in veranda that runs all the way around church

BAPTIZED
Baptism in water was a sign of converting to Christianity. People wore the white baptismal clothes for a week after the ceremony.

CHRIST THE TRIUMPHANT KING
The most powerful symbol of Christianity is Christ on the cross. Scandinavian artists interpreted it in their own way. This crucifix comes from Åby in Jutland, Denmark. It is made of carved oak covered in sheets of gilded copper. Christ is shown as a king wearing a crown. His eyes are wide open, and only his hands have nail holes. He looks triumphant, not suffering.

CNUT THE GREAT
Born in Denmark, Cnut invaded England in 1016. By 1028, he was king of Denmark, England, and Norway. Though he took England by the sword, he was a Christian king who built churches to make up for the bloody raids of his Viking ancestors.

Collar

Hair hangs down in long braids

Only hands are nailed to cross

Early Scandinavian cross from Birka, Sweden

Knee-length tunic tied in place with cords

AWAY, DEVILS!
Ringing church bells to call people to church was an important way of shpwing official Christianity. These bell-ringers are woven on a 12th-century tapestry from Skog church in Sweden (p. 52). They are thought to be ringing the bells to keep the old gods away.

Cross

Thor's hammer

Cross

BEST OF BOTH WORLDS
The old gods did not die overnight. This stone mold from Himmerland in Denmark shows that craftsmen were happy to make Thor's hammers and Christian crosses at the same time. Many Christian Vikings kept their faith in Thor, just in case.

ADAM AND EVE
Scandinavian craftsmen soon started depicting scenes from the Bible as well as dragons and Viking legends. This stone carving from Skara church in Sweden shows Adam and Eve being expelled from Paradise.

Index

Acknowledgments

Dorling Kindersley would like to thank:
Birthe L. Clausen at the Viking Ship Museum, Roskilde, Denmark; Vibe Ødegaard and Niels-Knud Liebgott at the National Museum of Denmark, Copenhagen; Brynhilde Svenningsson at the Vitenskapsmuseet, Univ. of Trondheim, Norway; Arne Emil Christensen and Sjur H. Oahl at the Viking Ship Museum, Oslo, Norway; Lena Thalin-Bergman and Jan Peder Lamm at the Statens Historika Museum, Stockholm, Sweden; Patrick Wallace and Wesley Graham at the National Museum of Ireland, Dublin; Elizabeth Hartley at York Museum & Christine McDonnel & Beverly Shaw at York Archaeological Trust, England; Dougal McGhee; Claude & Mimi Carez; Niels & Elizabeth Bidstrup in Copenhagen and Malinka Briones in Stockholm for their warm hospitality; Norse Film and Pageant Society; Helena Spiteri for editorial help; Manisha Patel and Sharon Spencer for design help.
Additional photography: Geoff Dann (models 12, 13, 19, 27, 28, 30, 31, 44 and animals 37, 38–39); Per E. Fredriksen (32bl, 32–33); Gabriel Hildebrandt at the Statens Historika Museum, Stockholm; Janet Murray at the British Museum, London.
Illustrations: Simone End, Andrew Nash
Index: Céline Carez

Picture credits
a=above, b=below, c=center, l=left, r=right
Archeological & Heritage Picture Library, York: 16bc; Bibliothèque Nationale, Paris: 16br; Biofoto, Frederiksberg/Karsten Schnack: 20cl, /JK Winther: 22cr; Bridgeman Art Library, London/Jamestown-Yorktown Foundation/©M Holmes: 21tl, /Musée d'Art Moderne, Paris/Giraudon, Wassily Kandinsky "Song of the Volga" 1906, © ADAGP, Paris and DACS, London 1994: 19br, /Russian Museum, St Petersburg, © Ilya Glazunov "The Grandsons of Gostomysl": 18bl; British Museum: 2bc, 4cal, 5bc, 6cr, 14c, 16cl, 25tr, 27cl, 29bl, 29br, 36bc, 37cl, 46tl, 46c, 47c 2nd out, 47br, 48bl, 49tr, 59cr 4th down; Jean-Loup Charmet, Paris: 6tl, 10tl, 16c, 19tr, 34tl, 38br; DAS Photo: 55cl; C.M. Dixon: 12br, 53cr, /Museum of Applied Arts, Oslo: 13tl; Mary Evans Picture Library: 14cr, 17tc, 20tl, 30tl, 46bc, 53cl, 53br; Fine Art Photographs: 57bl, Forhistorisk Museum, Moesgård: 52br; Werner Forman Archive: 21tr, 24br, /Arhus Kunstmuseum, Denmark: 53tl, /Statens Historiska Museum: 52cr, 63br, /Universitetets Oldsaksamling, Oslo: 43cl; Michael Holford/ Nasjonalgalleriet, Oslo 1993/J Lathion: Christian Krohg "Leiv Eirikson discovering America" oil on canvas (313 x 470cm): 24tr, Johannes Flintoe "The Harbour at Skiringssal" oil on canvas (54 x 65 cm) (detail): 28bl; National Maritime Museum: 24cal, /James Stephenson: 25car; Nationalmuseet, Copenhagen/Kit Weiss: 29tr, 29c, 44br; National Museum of Ireland: 7cr, 16tr, 17tr, 50cr, 59tr 2nd down; Peter Newark's Historical Pictures: 11cl, 17cl; Novosti /Academy of Sciences, St. Petersburg: 22tr; © Pierpont Morgan Library, New York 1993 M736 f 9v: 7bl, f 12v: 17tl; Mick Sharp: 38tr; Statens Historiska Museum, Stockholm / Bengt Lundberg: 28tl; TRIP: 32tr, 57tl; Universitets Oldsaksamling, Oslo: 8tr, 9tl, 13tr, 13cl, 25tc, 32cr, 43cl, 51c, 55tl, 55tr, 55cr; Vikingeskibs-hallen Roskilde/Werner Karrasch: 11tc; Vitenskapsmuseet, University of Trondheim/ Per Fredriksen: 30cl, 32bl, 32/33b; Eva Wilson: 59br.

Every effort has been made to trace the copyright holders. Dorling Kindersley apologizes for any unintentional omissions and would be pleased, in such cases, to add an acknowledgment in future editions.